BABYSITTING NIGHTMARES

THE SHADOW HAND

WITHDRAWN

KAT SHEPHERD

ILLUSTRATED BY RAYANNE VIEIRA

[Imprint]
MAKE YOUR MARK

New York

[Imprint]
MAKE YOUR MARK

A part of Macmillan Publishing Group, LLC
175 Fifth Avenue, New York, NY 10010

BABYSITTING NIGHTMARES: THE SHADOW HAND. Text copyright © 2018 by Katrina
Knudson. Illustrations copyright © 2018 by Imprint. All rights reserved.
Printed in the United States of America by
LSC Communications, Harrisonburg, Virginia.

Library of Congress Cataloging-in-Publication Data is available.

ISBN 978-1-250-15696-9 (hardcover) / ISBN 978-1-250-15697-6 (ebook)

Our books may be purchased in bulk for promotional, educational, or business
use. Please contact your local bookseller or the Macmillan Corporate and
Premium Sales Department at (800) 221-7945 ext. 5442 or by e-mail
at MacmillanSpecialMarkets@macmillan.com.

Book design by Eileen Savage

Imprint logo designed by Amanda Spielman

Illustrated by Rayanne Vieira

First edition, 2018

1 3 5 7 9 10 8 6 4 2

mackids.com

If you should choose to steal this tome
The Nightmare Queen shall claim your home
With mushrooms foul and fungus fey
And bathe your room in sweet decay.
So take for keeps what should be loans
And feel her curse upon your bones!

To Eddie, who inspired me to start
And to Elly, who made sure that I finished

CHAPTER
1

REBECCA CHIN DUG her fingernails into her palms, dreading what would happen next. In the darkness, she could hear something creeping down the alley. Heavy, dragging footsteps splashed through the dirty puddles that filled the alley's potholes, and the streetlight above illuminated a hunched, misshapen silhouette lurching along the wall. A scaly claw scraped across the brick as the shadow turned the corner and loomed larger, filling her vision. Rebecca pressed her hand against her mouth and bit down on her knuckles, stifling a moan. She curled herself into a tight ball and squeezed her eyes shut, praying for the moment to be over. Where was the creature now? Had it reached the end of the alley? Her ears strained for movement, but the air was silent . . . until something crept up behind her and icy, liquid fingers slithered down her neck.

She screamed.

Whirling around, Rebecca found a snickering Maggie standing behind the couch, her green eyes sparkling with mischief. Maggie's ruddy, round cheeks broke into a grin and she tucked her hand behind her back, but not before Rebecca noticed the melting ice cubes dripping between her fingers.

"Not funny!" Rebecca mopped at her neck with the collar of her plaid flannel shirt. Her olive skin was pink and blotchy where the ice had chilled it. "Are you trying to give me a heart attack? Watching horror movies is bad enough without your trying to scare me, too! You know how freaked out I get."

"Of course I know," Maggie said. "That's what makes it so fun!"

"I tried to stop her," Tanya said, picking up the remote, "but she wouldn't listen. As usual." She

paused the movie and stretched, reaching for the light switch on the wall behind her. Her usually tawny arms were tanned to a darker brown, evidence of a summer spent outside.

Maggie flipped her auburn curls and shrugged a freckled shoulder. "Listening is boring," she said, "and no one will ever accuse me of being boring."

"Of course not," Tanya said. "The list of things we could accuse you of is so long, I don't think there's room to add anything else." Maggie laughed and took a bow.

Rebecca and Tanya exchanged a knowing smile and picked up their glasses of ice water. Before Maggie knew what was happening, her two friends slid several ice cubes down the back of her gold-sequined tank top. She shrieked with laughter, twisting away.

Rebecca wiped her hands on her black leggings. "I see what you mean, Mags. That was the least boring thing I've done all day."

Maggie grimaced and squirmed as she shook out the ice cubes. "Where is Clio when I need her? She would have protected me from you two."

"Her aunt came yesterday, so she has to do family stuff," Tanya said. She brushed away the drops of water on her gray NASA T-shirt and ran her fingers over her bangs, smoothing her pixie-short hair back into place.

Rebecca had known Maggie and Tanya since preschool. The Chin family had just moved to the town of Piper then, and Rebecca still remembered nervously standing in the doorway of her new classroom, her yellow umbrella clutched in her hand. Tanya and Maggie had walked right over and asked her if she wanted to come and play Legos with them. Then cool, confident Clio had breezed into fourth grade one day, and the four girls had been inseparable ever since.

Rebecca slipped her feet into a pair of blue suede high-tops. "I actually have to get going. I'm babysitting."

"No way," Maggie said. "Friday Films are supposed to be sacred. Clio's already bailed, and it's only the third week of school. Now you, too?"

"Come on, Mags," Tanya said. "You know Clio feels bad, and she's already promised to bring the movie next week. Apparently her aunt has this huge collection, and she can borrow anything she wants."

Rebecca grabbed her cropped bomber jacket from the back of the couch. "Do you remember the first time she came over, and she brought that crazy movie about the giant turtle monster?"

"*Gammera the Invincible*," Tanya said. "That was the best!"

Maggie folded her arms and smirked. "Fine, okay. Clio's awesome. She gets a pass for today. So what's your excuse, Becks?"

"Kyle's mom asked me to start a little earlier tonight."

"Wow, Kyle again?" Maggie asked.

Rebecca nodded. "He's almost a year old now, and he's cuter every day."

"Is he still BFFs with his teddy bear?" Tanya asked. "I remember when I filled in for you, he wouldn't let it out of his sight!"

"He's finally old enough to bring it into his crib with him, and his parents haven't been able to wash it since," Rebecca said.

Maggie wrinkled her nose. "You say that like it's a good thing. Yuck!"

"Come on, it's not that bad. Besides, he's such a sweet baby! If a grungy teddy bear is the worst thing I have to deal with, I'll take it." Rebecca zipped up her jacket. "Sorry I have to go so early. Hey, Mags, don't forget to put the dishes in the sink when you guys finish the movie. Your mom got so mad last time when you forgot."

Maggie rolled her eyes. "Thanks, Mom Number Two. I think I got it covered."

Rebecca laughed. She slung on her caramel leather backpack and headed up the basement stairs to the front porch, Tanya and Maggie trailing behind her.

"I haven't forgiven you for bailing on us yet!" Maggie called as Rebecca strapped on her helmet and climbed onto her bike.

Tanya shook her head and threw her arm around Maggie's shoulder. "Such a drama queen! Call if you need us, 'kay?"

Rebecca smiled. "With Kyle? I doubt it, but thanks!" She pedaled off toward the Dunmores' house, her mind already filling with thoughts of the night's babysitting.

Rebecca and her friends had taken a babysitting course at the library together in fifth grade, and she had received her CPR certification when she started middle school last year. Although she had been looking after her little brother, Isaac, for years, the Dunmores had been her first real clients. She had started out as Mrs. Dunmore's helper when Kyle was just a few weeks old, assisting her with household chores, changing diapers, and learning to feed the baby with a bottle. Over time Mrs. Dunmore had let Rebecca stay alone with him while she ran short errands, and now Rebecca was the babysitter for the couple's regular date nights.

· · · · ·

Soon Rebecca parked her bike in the garage of the Dunmores' brown-shingled house and walked up the steps to the front porch.

A squeal of happiness erupted from inside the house when Rebecca rang the bell. A tall, sandy-haired woman opened the door, holding a chubby baby with bright blue eyes. He reached out for his babysitter. "He got so excited when he saw you through the front window!" Mrs. Dunmore said.

Rebecca lifted him toward her, and he snuggled against her chest. She tilted her face down to catch his eye. "I missed you, too, sunshine."

Kyle whimpered, and Mrs. Dunmore handed him the well-loved teddy bear she had been holding. "Don't worry; Bearbear's right here." He clutched it tightly against his chest.

"Still inseparable, huh?" Rebecca asked.

"I've already resigned myself to Bearbear being in Kyle's college graduation photos." Rebecca laughed and followed Mrs. Dunmore into the kitchen.

She opened the refrigerator door and said, "Kyle's had his dinner, but help yourself to anything."

Mr. Dunmore ducked his head into the kitchen. "We made the lasagna that you love, so be sure to grab a piece or two." Kyle broke into a huge smile and reached for his father's wavy brown hair.

Mr. Dunmore's blue eyes twinkled as he looked

down at his son. "Be good for your favorite sitter."

Mrs. Dunmore moved closer for a family hug. "I know we're probably biased, but I'm pretty sure he's the best baby in the entire world."

Rebecca grinned. "You may be biased, but yes, he obviously wins the Number One Baby Award. Have a great time tonight."

. . . . .

A few hours later, Rebecca put away the last of the plastic blocks and scooped Kyle up from the blanket she had spread over the floor. "I think we've done enough building for tonight, sunshine. It's time for bed." Holding him in her arms, she bent over to pick up a stray block and tossed it into the toy box with a clatter. Kyle laughed in surprise and gnawed on Bearbear's ear. They made their way slowly up the stairs to his bedroom.

After they sat in the rocking chair to read his favorite bedtime book about animal families, Rebecca stood and carried Kyle to the window. Dusk had fallen, shading the backyard and forest beyond in soft, deep grays. Kyle waved to something below, his chubby fingertips brushing against the glass. Rebecca squeezed him, smiling. "Are you saying good night to your animal friends?" She peered into the dark space between the trees to see what had caught his eye, but nothing was there. The full moon sat heavy on the horizon, a few pinpoints of stars beginning to dot the deepening sky above.

Rebecca settled Kyle and Bearbear into the crib and began to sing, her off-key voice wavering: "*By the light of the silvery moon . . .*" When Rebecca was younger, she would already be tucked in bed by the time her parents came home from work, but they would always come in to kiss her good night and sing the same corny old tune. Now it was Kyle's favorite lullaby, too. "*Your silvery beams will bring love dreams . . . by the light of the moon.*" Her voice cracked on the high note, and Kyle giggled sleepily, his eyelids already closing.

A short time later, Rebecca sat at the kitchen table, leafing through a cookbook and savoring her last bites of lasagna. The baby monitor was on, and she could hear Kyle's soft, even breathing with that tiny hint of a snuffle he always had.

As she brought her plate to the sink, she was surprised to hear the rumble of thunder—the forecast hadn't called for rain.

Rebecca jumped as a flash of lightning lit up the sky and a clap of thunder shook the house. Sheets of rain pounded the roof.

Violent storms like this were rare in Oregon; Rebecca still remembered watching one roll through, back before her little brother, Isaac, was born. The power had gone out; her parents had lit candles and the three of them had played cards on the screened porch, smelling the rain and watching the light show in the sky.

She thought back to the emergency section of her babysitting course. Maggie's constant jokes had made even the instructor laugh and lose track of her lecture, much to Rebecca's frustration, but all the girls had still done well on the final test to earn their certificates.

Flashlights, she thought, walking to the kitchen's

utility drawer. She pulled out two and clicked them on and off. On the monitor, the baby's even breathing had changed to a sleepy babbling. Kyle wasn't scared, but it sounded like the thunder had woken him up.

The lights flickered. She remembered a cool camping trick that Tanya had taught her, something about using a flashlight and a water bottle to make a lantern. Rebecca picked up her phone and sent a quick text:

> What was that camping lantern thing you showed me?

> W/the H2O bottle?

Rebecca grinned. Classic science-obsessed Tanya, writing *H2O* instead of just *water*. The other day she had texted: *GTG. NdGT is on.* It had taken Rebecca forever to figure out *NdGT* stood for Neil deGrasse Tyson, host of the TV show *Cosmos*. Who else but Tanya would have a special shorthand for an astrophysicist?

Yeah

Shine flashlight against full bottle. Works lk a lantern.

Thx! Crazy storm!

???

Rebecca was about to text back when the sky flashed bright white and the electricity went out, shrouding the house in darkness. There was a deafening clap of thunder, and everything fell silent. Rebecca froze and let her eyes adjust. She listened for Kyle's cries. Had the thunder woken him up? That was when she realized that the baby monitor had fallen silent, too.

Rebecca turned on a flashlight, shoving her phone in her pocket as she raced up the stairs. Kyle's baby monitor ran on batteries, so the storm shouldn't affect it. Something was wrong.

Rebecca ran to Kyle's room. She paused in the doorway and shone the flashlight across the crib.

She couldn't see Kyle. Her breath hitched. She walked carefully over to the crib and slowly raised the flashlight. There was a dark shape in the corner of the crib—Kyle. He was asleep, curled up like an animal in its den. She shook her head, feeling silly for worrying. *Of course he's in his crib. Where else would he be?* She glanced at the monitor, noticing that the red indicator light was glowing. That meant that the battery was working up here. But it wasn't working downstairs. Weird.

She reached in and gently moved Kyle to the center of the mattress, careful not to wake him. Her forehead wrinkled in confusion. Bearbear wasn't in its usual spot in the crib—Bearbear was *always* in the crib at night; Kyle refused to sleep unless he could see it at his feet.

Rebecca crouched down and peered under the crib. In her unsteady hand, the light swept wildly against the wall, stretching the shadows of the room. From behind her she heard the soft creak of the rocker, and she turned and pointed the beam at the empty chair. It sat as still as a stone. But on the floor nearby, she noticed a familiar shape:

Bearbear. "How did you get all the way over here?" she whispered, picking up the toy. It was damp and clammy, like it had been outside.

That was when she noticed the open window. The hair stood up on her neck. It hadn't been open earlier; she was sure of it. She remembered how Kyle's hand had streaked the glass when he had waved to something in the woods below. The window had definitely been closed. And locked. A sharp gust of wind swept through the room, pushing dead leaves against the outside of the screen. *Could the wind have blown the window open?* Rebecca hugged Bearbear to her chest and looked back at Kyle. *Wind can't blow open a locked window.* She swallowed the rising lump of fear in her throat.

Rebecca put Bearbear safely back in Kyle's crib and closed the window, locking it securely. Her hands grazed the windowsill, brushing against something cold and slimy. Rebecca recoiled. What had earlier been a clean white windowsill now had a layer of moss on it. And the moss was in the shape of a hand.

CHAPTER 2

REBECCA DROPPED THE flashlight, plunging the room back into darkness. Heart pounding, she bent down and fumbled around on the carpet, searching frantically for the flashlight. Her breath sounded loud and ragged in her ears. She could feel eyes watching her, like someone was hiding in the room, waiting to pounce.

Finally, her trembling hands closed over the familiar metal cylinder and she clicked it on, sweeping the beam across the room. No one was there.

She forced herself to think. A person would need a ladder. He or she would make a lot of noise and probably leave muddy footprints from the rain outside. But *something* had come in the house.

She knelt by the sill and shone the light on the print, examining it closely. *What would leave a handprint like that?* The palm was much smaller than her own, but the fingers were long and thin. The storm had been loud and sudden. Maybe a frightened animal had come inside to hide. *Could a raccoon have gotten in here?*

Rebecca scanned the room, listening for scratching or chittering. There were no animal tracks in the room, and there was no sign that anything had been disturbed. Rebecca tried to organize her thoughts. *It probably heard me coming and ran back outside again.* She headed toward the hallway. *But maybe I should check the rest of the upstairs, just in case.*

From the doorway, she heard a rustling sound in Kyle's crib and jumped. *The raccoon!* She turned and saw Kyle grabbing for Bearbear. She let out a long breath, embarrassed. *It's just Kyle loving on his teddy bear.* Except instead of pulling his toy closer, he tossed it out of the crib onto the floor.

Rebecca bent over the crib and picked up the stuffed bear. "What's wrong?" she asked Kyle, placing the toy at his feet again. "Go back to sleep, sunshine." She glanced out the window and saw that the rain had stopped. "The storm's over now. There won't be any more noisy thunder to wake you up." Rebecca bent to kiss Kyle good night, noticing that he had kicked the bear into the farthest corner of the crib.

The lights flickered on, reminding Rebecca to finish her search for any runaway wildlife. As she ducked into the Dunmores' bedroom, she pulled out her phone to give them a quick update. With all the thunder and lightning, they must have been worried about the power going out. In fact, she was surprised they hadn't called to check in.

She was peering under the linen bed skirt, scanning for animals, when Mrs. Dunmore picked up. "Hi, Mrs. Dunmore. Sorry for disturbing your dinner, but I just wanted to call to let you know that everything is fine here. The power went out for a few minutes, but I found the flashlights, and anyway, it's already back on. Can you believe Kyle slept through the whole thing?" She peeked into the master bathroom.

"Wait, the electricity went out?" Mrs. Dunmore sounded surprised. "Thanks for keeping a cool head. I wonder what made it go out, though. Was there a crew working on the power lines or something?"

"No, I'm sure it was because of the storm. It came on pretty fast and loud." She moved down the hallway to the guest room and did a quick search. No critters.

There was a long pause on the line. "What storm?" Mrs. Dunmore asked.

Rebecca moved back to Kyle's room to check one last time. "There was a really big storm not too long ago. Tons of thunder and lightning and just pouring rain. It even blew open one of the windows." Rebecca poked uneasily at the mark on the windowsill. "I'm surprised you didn't hear it from the restaurant."

"That's what I'm so confused about," Mrs. Dunmore replied. "It was so nice out that Scott and I ate outside on the restaurant's patio. There hasn't been a cloud in the sky here all night."

CHAPTER 3

"*I STILL CAN'T* believe that none of you heard that storm last weekend," Rebecca said, closing her gym locker. "It was intense!" She smoothed her French braid and poked a few stray golden-brown strands back into place.

"Oh yeah, a storm so intense that no one else saw it. Woooo, spooky *moss*!" Maggie joked. She bent over her rhinestone-covered backpack, searching for the zipper.

Rebecca narrowed her brown eyes, irritated with Maggie's teasing. "Look, I'm telling you, if you had been there, you would have lost it. That print looked exactly like a little hand with skinny, long fingers. Any minute I could have found myself face-to-face with some freaked-out raccoon or who-knows-what! Besides, don't you think it's even a little strange that a *locked* window was open all of a sudden?"

"Did you at least get to use the water bottle lanterns?" Tanya asked, hoping to stave off an argument between her two headstrong friends.

"No, the power came back on before I had a chance to." Rebecca pulled her phone out of her pocket and tapped on the calendar. "Clio, are you sure you're okay with babysitting Kyle next Saturday afternoon while I'm at my baking class?"

Clio tightened the elastic around one of her Afro puffs and slipped her deep bronze feet into a pair of studded leather sandals. "Definitely," she said, shrugging her vintage jean jacket over her striped sailor shirt and coral print skirt. "I've heard so much about this li'l cuddlebug; I'm dying to meet him!"

"But aren't you scared, too? I mean, what if

there's another *storm?*" Maggie asked sarcastically. Rebecca's face darkened, and she opened her mouth for a sharp retort.

"What's the baking class this time?" Tanya asked quickly. She reached under the long wooden bench to pick up a stray silver sneaker.

"Fondant," Rebecca answered. "It's this icing that's like a sheet you lay over the cake for decoration. It tastes kind of gross, but it looks so amazing that it's worth it."

"Nothing is worth a gross-tasting cake, Becks. I mean . . . it's cake. Why mess with perfection?" Maggie looked across the bench to see Tanya waving the shoe she'd found. "That's mine!" she chirped.

"Of course it's yours." Tanya turned it over and showed Maggie what was written on the sole: *Maggie Anderson Lost This.* "Wow, your mom's really getting creative with the labeling."

"I think she's running out of ideas. I lost my math binder last week and didn't realize it was missing until yesterday," Maggie said.

"Oh, Maggie, not again," Rebecca said. "I color-code all my stuff by class, and it makes it really easy to stay organized. Do you want me to help you do the same thing?"

"Nope!" Maggie slammed her gym locker with a flourish and turned to Tanya. "Hey, T, can I borrow your math notes to make sure mine are caught up?"

"Sure," Tanya said. She unzipped an army-green canvas backpack covered in buttons and pins, then pulled out a binder with a *peace. love. math.* bumper sticker on the front cover. "Just get them back to me before school tomorrow."

Maggie crammed the binder into her overflowing backpack. "Thanks."

Rebecca watched the two of them for a moment before Clio tapped her on the shoulder. "Hey, what time next Saturday?" Clio asked, holding up her phone to check the calendar. Her latest phone case looked like the Rosetta stone. Her parents were history and archaeology professors at the local university, and the family had picked it out together on a summer trip to London.

"From twelve until four thirty," Rebecca answered. She couldn't help envying Clio, who always seemed to have so much fun with her family. Last year the Carter-Petersons had spent the summer hiking through Peru and visiting Machu Picchu. Rebecca's parents were doctors who shared a busy private practice. When the Chin family had gone to Boston last year, her parents had planned a "special surprise" during their trip. Rebecca wasn't sure what she had been hoping for—maybe one of those cool private bakery tours that she'd read about online—but it certainly wasn't a visit to the Warren Anatomical Museum. She had never known that something so boring could also be so disgusting.

"Thanks a ton for covering. I'll e-mail you all the info about his routines and stuff. I'll have my phone, so you can call if you have any problems. But he's honestly so easy, I can't imagine you'll need to."

"Sounds perfect," Clio said, sliding her phone into the pocket of her multicolored embroidered backpack. Rebecca, Clio, Tanya, and Maggie left the locker room and walked outside just as the final bell rang. It was a perfect September day: fluffy white clouds dotting the bright blue sky, the sun shining. Maggie turned to the other girls. "Do you want to go get ice cream?"

"I wish. But I'm saving up for a new phone," Tanya said. Tanya's phone was inherited from her older brother, Bryce. Even after she removed all of his weird gamer apps, it was still painfully slow, and the camera was broken.

"I didn't bring any money today, either," Rebecca said.

"I can't right now. I promised my auntie I'd help her at her new costume shop. She just moved here from LA last Thursday, and the whole place is one big pile of boxes right now," Clio said. "Do you guys want to come? It's actually pretty fun; she has all these amazing clothes and a ton of really weird stuff to go through. If we help unpack, she'll probably buy ice cream for all of us."

"Costumes . . . ice cream . . . solid plan," Maggie said.

A few minutes later, the girls walked down Coffin Street—an eclectic block of artsy little shops and cafés, modern-looking offices, and several older wooden buildings with peeling paint and FOR RENT signs in the windows. "We're here," Clio said, stopping in front of a faded white structure. Rebecca had pictured a shop like the ones that popped up at the mall every October, with bright lights, fluorescent orange signs, and inflatable ghosts. But this shop was nothing like that. The windows were so grimy with dust and cobwebs that Rebecca could barely see into the dimly lit building. A rusted sign that read ANTIQUES AND CURIOSITIES in faded, elegant lettering dangled precariously from one hook.

Rebecca reached up to tap the crooked sign, and it swayed dangerously. "I thought you said it was a costume shop," she said.

"It is now." Clio eyed the sign with frustration. "She was supposed to take that old sign down already." Turning back to the other girls, Clio explained, "This used to be a pawnshop or something, but the old lady who owned it died a few months back, and everything was left inside. The landlord didn't want to deal with clearing it out, so she told us we could keep anything we want."

"The old lady *died?*" Tanya said.

"Like, inside the shop?" Maggie said.

Clio shrugged. "I don't know. I doubt it, though. Hardly anyone came in here. I don't think it was open that much."

Maggie shuddered. "But she might have. She could have died right here, and nobody knew until some poor, unsuspecting stranger walked into that door and found a dead body. One that had been lying there for *days*. That is so creepy."

Clio rolled her eyes and pulled open the door. "It's not creepy. I've been here every day after school, and you won't believe all the cool old stuff I've found. Come on." Rebecca, Tanya, and Maggie followed reluctantly.

Rebecca was surprised to see how spacious it was inside. A few old floor lamps glowed faintly, illuminating a worn parquet floor covered in a patchwork of moth-eaten Persian rugs. Dress dummies stood like statues in between the empty clothing racks. Some were bare, while others were draped haphazardly in rich-looking fabrics. There was a skeleton next to a pile of blank, white Styrofoam heads, and ornately carved bookshelves lined the left wall, leading to a long glass counter stretched across the back of the store. Behind the counter, a doorway to a dark hallway interrupted a gallery of brooding antique portraits in gilded frames. And in the center of the room, there was a mountainous labyrinth of cardboard boxes.

"As you can see, we still have a lot of unpacking to do," Clio said. She peered over the boxes. "Auntie!" she called. "I brought some friends to help!" There was no answer. "She's probably in the back. Come on."

The other girls followed Clio through the narrow, maze-like path between the towers of boxes. Rebecca found herself keeping close to Clio, almost stepping on her heels. She could feel Tanya's breath on her neck. The boxes blocked out most of the shop's dim light, so Clio was little more than a shadow in front of her.

Without warning, Clio stopped short and Rebecca almost knocked her over. "Oof!" Rebecca grunted, as she felt the impact of both Tanya and Maggie bumping into her from behind.

"Sorry!" Tanya whispered. "I didn't know we were stopping."

"Neither did I," Rebecca whispered back. She peered over Clio's shoulder to see what had frozen her friend in her tracks.

There, behind the tower of boxes, lay the body of a woman.

CHAPTER 4

REBECCA SCREAMED, CAUSING a chain of screams behind her.

"What is it?!" Tanya shrieked.

"It's the dead lady!" Rebecca yelled.

"I knew it!" Maggie wailed. The shadowy form of the dead woman stirred, and the girls' screams grew louder.

Her arms rose straight into the air, and she slowly sat up, her sightless eyes staring forward. With lurching movements, the zombie rose to its feet. "Beware . . . ," it moaned in a throaty whisper.

Slow, shuffling steps led it closer and closer to the girls.

Clio's voice rose above the screams. "Very funny, Auntie! Now give it a rest; you're scaring my friends!"

The zombie stepped into the light. A twinkle appeared in her brown eyes, and her vacant expression sharpened into a delighted smile that lit up her coppery cheeks. "I'm sorry, y'all! I heard you talking outside, and I just couldn't help myself!" She brushed the dust off her well-worn jeans and soft, gray *Creature from the Black Lagoon* T-shirt. She adjusted the black head wrap around the dreadlocks that were knotted in a large bun at the top of her head, and Rebecca noticed her short nails were painted black with a pattern of lacy, white spiderwebs. "It's very nice to meet you, girls. I'm Clio's aunt, Kawanna Carter, and scaring you was the most fun I've had all day."

Rebecca sank to the floor in relief. "Oh my gosh. I've never been so terrified in my entire life," she gasped. Tanya and Maggie collapsed in giddy laughter.

"I almost peed my pants!" Maggie squealed.

"They came to help unpack, but I'm not sure they'll want to stay after that performance," Clio said. She folded her arms sternly, but a faint smile tugged at the corner of her mouth.

"I'm glad it was so convincing," Kawanna said. She picked up a red feather boa from off the floor and draped it around her neck, striking a dramatic pose. "I guess it means I still got it."

"Aunt Kawanna used to be an actress," Clio explained.

"Ooh, a star of stage and screen!" Maggie said. "That's my dream!"

"I was hardly a star." The woman laughed. "But I did manage to make it onto a few TV cop shows, and I was even in a Super Bowl commercial once! What I loved best, though, was acting in horror movies. I never get tired of making an audience jump."

"Obviously," Clio said drily.

Her aunt swatted her playfully. "Girl, you have always been way too serious!" She smiled at the other three girls. "Now let's get introduced properly so we can start unpacking."

An hour later, the shop looked far more cheerful. The mountain of boxes was slightly smaller, and one of the clothing racks was now a riot of color, from scarlet to gold to brilliant turquoise. Leather-bound books adorned one wooden shelf, and jewelry sparkled in a glass display case next to a row of multicolored wigs.

Rebecca nodded in satisfaction as she adjusted the collar of a purple velvet smoking jacket and hung it carefully on one of the racks. Across the shop, Maggie stood in front of a mannequin, smoothing the front of an intricate beaded poncho. She took a step back, then slipped a shaggy werewolf mask over the mannequin's head. Clio hovered over a silver tea tray, carefully laying out neat rows of plastic vampire fangs. Rebecca could just make out Tanya's head of sleek, dark hair bent over something near the bookshelves behind the counter.

"What did you find?" Rebecca called.

"Sorry; I keep getting distracted," Tanya said. "These books are so cool."

"You say that about every book! Which one is it this time?" Clio said, peering over the counter.

Tanya held up a slim red book. "It's called *Tales of the Night Queen*," Tanya replied. "It has all these crazy stories in it. There's a drawing in here of a guy with crickets jumping out of his mouth!"

"Oh, come on!" Maggie said. "Gross!"

"Sorry, Mags, but it's actually pretty interesting. And there's this other book here called *Ghostly Tales of Old Japan*. There's a whole chapter about fox spirits! Apparently that's a thing," Tanya said.

"Where did these books come from, anyway?" Rebecca asked. "Were they the old lady's?"

Kawanna poked her head out of the back hallway. "Hey! Who are you calling an old lady?"

"Sorry! I—I didn't mean you," Rebecca stammered. "I meant—"

"Don't mind her; she knows what you meant," Clio said, raising an eyebrow at her aunt. "She's just giving you a hard time."

"You girls just make it too easy." Kawanna laughed. "But to answer your question, some of the books are mine. I've been a horror fan since I was a little girl. But there was quite a large collection already here when I moved in." She walked over to Tanya and peered over her shoulder. "I'm still sorting through them. I thought I had everything, but there are some books here that I didn't even know existed—like that one." She pointed to the thin red book Tanya had been reading. "Will you leave it out for me? It sounds fascinating!" Her eyes widened as she took in the progress the girls had made while she had been working in the back office. "My goodness, what a difference. It almost looks like a real shop in here! Clio, your friends are welcome anytime. Now, who's ready for some ice cream to celebrate all this hard work?"

. . . . .

Rebecca finished the last of her peppermint cone with one loud crunch and wiped her hands with a crumpled napkin. Next to her, Clio licked a cone of wasabi-flavored ice cream and Tanya used her spoon to poke at the melted remains of her cup of vanilla peanut butter. Although Maggie had long since finished her cookie dough sundae, she was blissfully unaware of the sticky glob slowly melting in her red curls. Rebecca was unsurprised. *Typical*

Maggie. Rebecca leaned forward with a spare napkin. "Hey, Mags, you've got a little ice cream in your hair."

Maggie barely turned her head from her conversation with Kawanna. "Yeah, okay, thanks," she answered, absently grabbing the napkin and waving Rebecca away as though she were a troublesome insect.

Embarrassed, Rebecca glanced at the other girls to see if they had noticed the brush-off, and she was grateful to hear them talking quietly about an upcoming history test. She knew Maggie was kind of moody sometimes, but usually not in front of an adult. Of course, Kawanna wasn't exactly a typical adult. How many adults went around pretending to be dead to prank their niece's friends? Rebecca stifled a giggle, remembering how she and Maggie and Tanya had scrambled around, screaming and pawing at one another.

Kawanna peered past Maggie to Rebecca, and her smile widened. "What are you laughing about over there all by yourself?"

Rebecca grinned. "I just keep thinking about

us freaking out and falling all over each other this afternoon. You really got us."

"You should have seen your face!" Maggie said to Rebecca. "I wish someone could have filmed it!"

"What about yours?" Tanya challenged. "I thought your eyes were going to pop right out of your head and roll between those boxes, they were so bugged out!"

Clio smirked. "I don't know what you were thinking! Like I would invite you all into some haunted house or something? And do you really think a ghost would be dressed like *that*?" She pointed at the feather boa her aunt still wore around her neck.

"Like you've never seen a ghost with a feather boa before?" Kawanna asked, straightening in her chair.

"Please don't get started on the ghost thing," Clio answered. "They don't want to hear it."

"Now, I wouldn't be too sure about that, Li'l Bit," Kawanna shot back. She turned to the other girls. "We were shooting a movie in an old mansion once, and I swear I saw some things that you wouldn't believe."

Maggie's eyes widened with curiosity. "Like what?" she whispered.

Kawanna lowered her voice, and the girls drew nearer. "Well, the house had been abandoned for years before we got there, and it always felt like someone was watching us if we were on our own there late at night. But we just laughed about it, you know, joking the creepy feelings away." She leaned in closer, her voice now barely more than a whisper. "Then little things started to go missing. Someone's wig, a length of rope, things like that. Sometimes we would come in each morning to find props moved around, papers scattered every-where. Now, we had security guards patrolling the set twenty-four seven, so we know that nobody was getting into that mansion, and nobody was getting out."

Tanya quietly cleared her throat. "But maybe could it be . . ." Maggie shushed her quickly and scooted her chair closer to Kawanna.

"One night I had to stay late to organize the

costumes. I was the only one in the entire house. It was deathly quiet . . . but then I heard something downstairs. A ragged sliding, like something lurching across the floor. I heard a long, slow creak, and I knew someone, or something, had opened the basement door."

"How did you know it was the basement door?" Tanya asked.

"Shhh!" Maggie put her hand over Tanya's mouth.

"I crept downstairs. The basement door was open a few inches. Most of the lights were off . . . all I could see was inky blackness through the doorway, but I could *hear* something. Like a raspy hiss, followed by a thud. *Hiss . . . thud. Hiss . . . thud.* Something was being dragged slowly down the stairs."

Rebecca hugged herself.

"I was terrified, but I made myself walk to that open door. I had to know what it was. Slowly, slowly, I opened the door. The sound below stopped. I waited. A few minutes later it started again. *Hiss . . . thud. Hiss . . . thud.* I jumped forward and turned on the light. There, in the middle of the stairs, was a human head."

The girls collectively gasped, and Rebecca dropped her napkin.

"It was just one of our props; it wasn't a real human head," Kawanna said, and Clio swatted her arm. "But it wasn't moving by itself," Kawanna whispered. "Something was pulling it by the hair."

Rebecca leaned forward, perching on the edge of her chair. "What was it?" she whispered.

Kawanna gestured for the girls to lean in even closer, until the tops of their heads were almost touching.

"A RAT!" Kawanna shouted, and the girls jumped, knocking their trash off the table. "Turns out the whole house was infested with them. We had to hire an exterminator before we could finish shooting the movie."

The girls laughed and bent to gather their trash. Clio tossed a plastic spoon into the garbage can, shaking her head. "You are too much, Auntie."

"Oh, those poor rats," Tanya said, and Rebecca patted her back. Rebecca still remembered the day in preschool when Tanya had learned where bacon came from and immediately declared herself a vegetarian.

"Trust me, if you had seen how big those rats were, you wouldn't be feeling sorry for them," Kawanna said. "They were scarier than any ghost would ever be!"

Rebecca giggled along with the others, but the story made her think back to Kyle's room on the night of the storm—the way the wind had pushed the autumn leaves against the window screen. The handprint. The feeling of something watching. Maybe the wind had blown open the window, but she was sure the print on the sill had been left by . . . something. An animal? But how would an animal have gotten through the screen?

CHAPTER 5

"*THANKS AGAIN FOR* coming on such short notice," Mrs. Dunmore said, slinging a bulging tote bag onto her shoulder. "I know you have school tomorrow, so it's only for a little while. I'm heading to Book Club and Scott got held up at work. He should be home in less than an hour." Rebecca didn't usually babysit for the Dunmores on Wednesdays, but she had been happy to bike over when Mrs. Dunmore called earlier in the evening.

Rebecca looked down at her watch. "Kyle's already had dinner, but does he need a bath before bed?"

Mrs. Dunmore smiled. "Nope, that's done, too! I wanted it to be as easy as possible for you tonight."

"Sounds good to me!" Rebecca said. She scooped the baby up in her arms. "You ready to play, sunshine?" She paused and looked up at Mrs. Dunmore. "Wait a minute, where's Bearbear?"

"Bearbear . . . ?" Mrs. Dunmore looked confused for a moment, and then her face lit up with recognition. "That's right," she answered. "Kyle doesn't seem that interested in Bearbear anymore."

Rebecca's eyes widened in surprise. "Wow. I mean, that was fast. What happened?"

Mrs. Dunmore's smile faded a bit as she tried to think. "I don't really know. I think it was around the time you last babysat, when Scott and I went to that adorable new restaurant. Something kind of funny happened that night, didn't it? Something with the power lines. Do you remember?"

Stunned, Rebecca felt her mouth drop open in shock. Of course she did; it had been less than two weeks ago! "Yeah, there was that weird big storm and the power went out."

"Is that what happened?" Mrs. Dunmore asked vaguely. "Anyway, I think it was around then."

Rebecca was floored. Kyle and Bearbear had been inseparable, but now Mrs. Dunmore didn't seem to care that Kyle had suddenly outgrown his toy. It was strange—Rebecca's own parents still took every opportunity possible to tell the story of their daughter throwing her pacifier out the car window. "Wow, big change! How is he doing with it?"

Mrs. Dunmore's eyes shifted into focus again. "Well, he's been a little . . . off . . . the last few days. Nothing major, just kind of fussy. We wondered if he might be teething again." She stroked her son's cheek and put the tote bag back on the floor. "Maybe I should stay. . . ."

"If you want to stay home, I'm happy to stick around and help," Rebecca offered. "But I think we'll be fine. I can always pull out the jelly ring from the freezer if it gets too bad. It seemed to help the last time he got a tooth." She placed Kyle on a blanket spread over the carpet and handed him a plastic block.

After a few more reassurances and promises to call if anything went wrong, Rebecca gently herded Mrs. Dunmore out of the house and turned back to Kyle, who was playing idly with a vivid red maple leaf.

"Where did that come from?" Rebecca asked. She didn't remember seeing it when she had arrived—the bright splash of color would have been noticeable against the cool, neutral tones of the Dunmores' living room. The streamlined beige sofa and fluffy cream-colored rug blended gently into the pewter-gray walls. Even the photographs were in black and white. Feeling a sudden chill, Rebecca shivered and walked over to the open window. "I guess the wind blew it in," she said to the baby, forcing a note of cheer in her voice. She closed and locked the window, noticing a small, damp, green smudge on the otherwise sparkling glass pane. Her heart fluttered, but she pushed her anxious thoughts away. *It's just a smudge.*

Rebecca squatted down next to Kyle and reached for the leaf. "Can I see?" The baby giggled and pulled the treasure tightly to his chest, turning his body away from his sitter. "Well, fine, then." She laughed, shrugging.

Rebecca left Kyle with his leaf and wandered into the kitchen to pull his teething ring out of the freezer. In the silence of the house, Rebecca could hear whispers and giggles coming from the living room. Kyle babbled sometimes, but he knew only a few words, and she had certainly never heard him whisper. *I can't wait to tell his parents!* Rebecca thought, excited. "What are you talking about in there?" she called out happily, closing the freezer door.

The whispering stopped, and the giggling turned sly before it was cut off abruptly by a distinctive *Shh!*

Someone else was with Kyle.

Fear seized Rebecca's chest, and she dashed into the living room. The baby was alone, sitting on the blanket exactly where she had left him. She glanced around, sure she had heard whispers. Maybe Mr. Dunmore came home early and snuck into the house?

"Mr. Dunmore?" Rebecca called nervously. There was no answer. "Are you and Kyle trying to play a trick on me?" she asked doubtfully. He wasn't the kind of dad that usually played pranks, but who else would it be? She steeled herself, expecting him to jump out of the closet. Silent minutes ticked by. Rebecca checked the front door, just to be on the safe side. It was locked and bolted from the inside, just as she had left it. Then what had she heard?

Rebecca pulled her phone out of her pocket and tapped Maggie's name in her contacts. Even when they were little, Maggie had always had a knack for keeping Rebecca's worries from getting the best of her. The line rang twice, and then the call went to voice mail. "Hi, Mags," Rebecca said self-consciously. "It's me. I'm just feeling a little—" Rebecca remembered how Maggie had teased her about the storm. "Um . . . bored. So give me a call when you get this. Bye." Slipping the phone back in her pocket, she noticed Kyle watching her.

Rebecca picked up the baby and hugged him tightly to her chest. She thought back to a couple of years ago when her little brother, Isaac, had insisted that he shared his bedroom with an invisible snowman named Bartleby. Her brother had spent hours chattering away to Bartleby and drawing pictures of him. Isaac had been three then, but maybe babies could have imaginary friends, too.

"Were you talking with your new leaf friend?" Rebecca cooed, bouncing the baby gently as she walked. Kyle didn't answer, but his gaze was guarded when he looked up at her face. "You look sleepy," she said. "Let's get you to bed."

Rebecca carried Kyle slowly up the stairs and flicked on the hallway light. Family pictures lined the clay-colored walls. Faded old photos of the grandparents and great-grandparents hung next to a large wedding portrait of Mr. and Mrs. Dunmore kissing under a flower-covered arbor with a bright blue sky behind them. In another, the couple smiled proudly in a hospital room with a newborn Kyle swaddled up in their arms.

Continuing down the hall toward Kyle's room, Rebecca caught a faint whiff of a strange, earthy smell, like a forest floor after a rainstorm. She sniffed again, but the scent faded as quickly as it had come.

She reached inside Kyle's room and turned on the light, squinting against the sudden brightness. Why did his room look so grubby? Rebecca placed the baby in the crib and peered closely at the wall above it. The image was faint, but it looked like a series of little handprints. Rebecca smiled to herself. Kyle was probably using the edge of the crib to pull himself up and grabbing at the wall at night. He really was growing up.

She looked closer. The fingers of these prints seemed longer and skinnier than Kyle's short, stubby fingers. Maybe he had dragged his fingers along the wall . . . but the prints weren't streaky or smudgy. They had distinct, crisp outlines and seemed to go on much farther than just above Kyle's crib. In fact, they seemed to be all over the wall. She blinked.

Rebecca craned her neck. Was that them on the ceiling, too? The hair prickled on her scalp. It couldn't be.

She tried to imagine how the prints could have gotten there. Maybe Mr. Dunmore had been holding Kyle and letting him touch the ceiling for a game. Her stomach tightened. *You know those aren't Kyle's handprints.*

She thought of Kawanna's story about the rats. Maybe it was a raccoon after all. *But raccoons don't walk upside down on the ceiling.*

Rebecca pressed her body against the crib to brace herself as she stretched up on her tiptoes for a closer look.

Something brushed her shoulder. Rebecca yelped and whirled around.

"Rebecca, I'm so sorry! I didn't mean to scare you." Mr. Dunmore's face was sheepish. "I thought you heard me come in, and I didn't want to wake the baby." Kyle's eyelids fluttered, but his breathing stayed quiet and even.

Relieved, Rebecca caught her breath. "I'm sorry; I must not have heard you. I guess these handprints had me a little freaked out."

"Handprints?" he asked.

Rebecca pointed. Now that she knew they were there, the dirty marks showed up clearly against the pale blue paint of the wall. "I can understand how Kyle was able to get over here," she whispered,

gesturing toward the area near the crib, "but I'm not sure how he got to the rest of the wall, or up to the ceiling." Rebecca giggled. "Flying baby, maybe?"

Mr. Dunmore chuckled in disbelief. "Wow, I didn't notice how dirty the walls had gotten in here. Glad we splurged on the washable paint! I'll scrub these over the weekend." He squinted at the ceiling. "Must be cobwebs up there or something."

"No, not cobwebs." Rebecca pointed. "Look, see, they're handprints. I just wondered how they got there," she repeated, looking at him.

Mr. Dunmore met Rebecca's gaze, but his eyes were unfocused. "It doesn't look like handprints to me, but maybe your eyes are younger." He laughed and shrugged.

From behind him, Kyle's tiny hand snaked through the crib, and the red maple leaf fluttered down onto the carpet. "Oh, no, did we wake him?" Rebecca asked softly. Kyle's eyes were still closed, and he was curled up tightly. She bent to pick up the leaf. "Kyle wouldn't let go of it all night. Maybe it's his new Bearbear!"

"I'll take that," Mr. Dunmore said, reaching

out his hand. "Let's let him get back to sleep." He slipped the leaf into his pocket and stepped out of the room, switching off the light behind him.

Rebecca followed, peering uneasily back into the room one last time.

Her heart caught in her throat—a shadow moved from beneath Kyle's crib. In the blink of an eye, it scuttled across the wall and out through the open window.

CHAPTER 6

THIS MUST BE what heaven smells like, Rebecca thought as the smell of fresh vanilla cake permeated the warm air of the baking room. She brushed at her floury apron and admired her latest confectionary creation. Her cake nestled cozily in a white cardboard box, the pale yellow icing coating it like a velvety skin. Small, deep blue stars studded the top.

Sure, the fondant lumped a bit in a few spots, but it looked almost as good as any bakery cake. She gently closed the box's lid and tied it with cotton twine.

As she snipped off a length of twine, Rebecca was surprised to feel her phone buzzing insistently in her pocket. Her parents were at a medical seminar for the day, and her friends always texted. As soon as she saw Clio's name on the screen, a knot formed in the pit of her stomach.

"Hey, Clio. What's wrong?" Rebecca asked.

"Well, I don't know," her friend replied.

Rebecca cradled the phone against her ear. "What happened?"

"Kyle's acting really strange. He doesn't want to play any of the games you said he loves, and anytime I try to cuddle or pick him up, he throws a temper tantrum. He's been hitting me, too. I've tried everything, even singing his favorite lullaby, but nothing seems to calm him down."

"I'll be right over." Rebecca grabbed her helmet, hurried to her bike, and headed off to meet Clio.

Her mind turned over and over as she rode through the quiet, shady side streets that led to the Dunmores' neighborhood. Kyle had had other babysitters before, and she knew that Clio was a great sitter. What could be making him so upset?

He had certainly been crabby a few months ago when he had first started teething. And drooly. But he hadn't thrown tantrums. She thought about the shadow she had seen in his room and pedaled faster, pushing the memory from her mind. *That can't have been real.*

As Rebecca hauled her bike onto the Dunmores' porch, Clio opened the door to let her in. Rebecca noticed something white wrapped around Clio's hand. Kyle sat on the floor with his back to the girls, banging Bearbear with a green plastic hammer.

"How's he been acting since you called? Any better?" Rebecca asked.

Clio grimaced and held up her hand. "Not exactly."

"What's that?"

Clio sighed and gently began to unwind a white dishrag from around her hand. "He *bit* me. Hard, too! I'm bleeding." Bright red blood oozed out of a cut in the heel of her hand.

Rebecca bent over the wound. "Let me see." Remembering her first aid training, she examined it carefully without touching it. "It doesn't look very deep. Have you cleaned it?"

Clio shook her head. "I haven't had a chance. It just happened a few minutes ago, and I didn't want to leave Kyle alone. Thanks for coming over to help." Clio smiled gratefully at her friend and hurried off to the kitchen to clean her cut.

Rebecca turned to Kyle. "Hey, sunshine," she said softly. "What's going on?" The baby didn't look at her. She bent over and studied him. "C'mon, cuddlebug. What's wrong?" He didn't seem flushed or feverish. She reached for his forehead, and he smacked her hand away. Rebecca pulled back, stunned. "Whoa, Kyle. That's not how we act." Kyle hit his teddy bear a final time with the plastic hammer before shoving it away and crawling toward the coffee table.

"Not so fast, buddy," Rebecca said. She swooped down and picked him up. He twisted in her arms, a dark scowl on his face, and squealed furiously.

Clio walked back into the living room, a neon-blue bandage strip on her hand. "You're right; it wasn't very deep. But man, it really hurt!" She noticed the baby struggling in Rebecca's arms. "Yeah, that's exactly what he was doing with me. I can't figure out what's wrong with him! I thought it was because I was new, but I guess it's something else."

Kyle thrust his head and butted Rebecca's chin. Her head snapped back. "Ow!" she exclaimed.

Something dark flashed in Kyle's eyes, and a cruel giggle burbled out of him. Rebecca quickly walked Kyle over to his playpen and put him inside. "No, Kyle," she said. "We don't laugh when people get hurt." She turned to Clio, her eyes wide. "I don't understand what's gotten into him. I swear he is normally the sweetest, easiest baby on the planet! Last Wednesday was a strange night, but he barely fussed at all."

"Maybe it's just teething," Clio suggested. She held up her injured hand. "He's certainly got a few choppers in there."

"That's what I thought, too," Rebecca said slowly. "I mean, he has a few teeth already, so it would make sense that more are coming in. But, gosh, I just can't believe he *bit* you." She gazed worriedly at the playpen, where—one by one—Kyle methodically dropped each of his toys over the side and onto the living room floor. Purple plastic block. *Plop.* Stuffed giraffe. *Plop.* "Did Mr. and Mrs. Dunmore say anything about this before they left?"

"They told me he's been waking up at night a lot, and he seems hungrier than usual. And what was the word his mom used? *Ornery.* But I didn't expect I would be babysitting a piranha!"

Kyle sat in the empty playpen, looking out the window at the green trees beyond the yard. A shaft of sunlight lit up the playpen, bathing the baby in a soft glow, and he reached up, playing with the motes of dust that floated in the golden beam.

Rebecca watched the baby thoughtfully. "He seems okay now," she said. Rebecca bent over the playpen to check on him, and Kyle giggled and nipped at her hand. She heard his teeth snap together. Startled, she stumbled backward, losing her balance. She fell hard on her rear end. Kyle's snicker erupted into a shrieking laugh that curdled the air like spoiled milk.

Clio rushed over. "Rebecca! Are you hurt?"

Rebecca grimaced and shook her head. "I don't think so." The two girls looked back at Kyle, who clapped with spiteful delight.

As he let out another peal of laughter, he opened his mouth wide. Gleaming in the late afternoon sunlight were two new even rows of white, pointed teeth.

CHAPTER 7

REBECCA AND CLIO stared at each other, dumbstruck. "What *are* those?" Rebecca said, her voice sounding higher than intended.

"He didn't have them when I got here this afternoon," Clio said. "I swear he didn't."

"But how could they have grown in so fast? And why are they so pointy? That's not what baby teeth look like!"

"That's not what they feel like, either," Clio said.

Kyle sat calmly now, his eyes once again fixated on the greenery beyond the window.

"Kyle should only have about three or four teeth by now," Rebecca said. "And they shouldn't be pointy like this. He did already have a few teeth before, but they were just normal baby teeth."

She knelt down next to the playpen and gently reached out to stroke Kyle's fuzzy head. He ignored her but didn't move away.

"Something's been off since the night of that big storm," Rebecca said quietly.

Clio picked up a block and offered it hesitantly to the baby, who took it in his hand for a moment before letting it fall to the floor of the playpen. "That big storm that no one else remembers seeing or hearing . . . ," Clio replied. "Including his parents."

"It was a real storm!" Rebecca said fiercely. "Why would I make that up?"

"I'm not arguing with you," Clio answered. She eyed Kyle, who was watching them carefully, and dropped her voice. "But what if that freak storm is the reason for what's going on with Kyle?"

Clio and Rebecca looked at each other.

"I think it's time for your nap, little one,"

Rebecca said. She picked up Kyle cautiously and walked him upstairs to his room.

While she waited for him to settle, Rebecca walked to the window and idly flipped the lock back and forth, watching the curved pin slide out of the loop and then slide back in again. Soon she heard the baby's slow, even breathing. Something sounded different about it, and she realized she didn't hear his familiar snuffle. She ran her hand over the windowsill, where she could still see the ghost of a pale green handprint with reaching, narrow fingers.

"That's where you found the moss, right?" Clio whispered.

"Yeah, and look. It's still here. At least I think it is. It's hard to see it now."

Clio came closer and peered at the windowsill. "It *does* look like a handprint," she replied, "only it's smaller than a person's hand, and the fingers are way longer."

"Yeah, and it's exactly the shape of the other handprints that were all over the room when I was here on Wednesday. Mr. Dunmore scrubbed them all off, though." Rebecca shifted. "I don't think he really believed me that they were handprints. I didn't even try to tell him about the shadow I thought I saw." Rebecca quickly explained what she had seen the last time she was at the Dunmores'.

Clio shivered and walked toward the door. "What was the shadow like?"

Rebecca followed. "I don't know. Small. Kind of . . . monkey-shaped, I guess? I only saw it for a second. I tried to tell myself it was just my imagination." She paused, looking back at the quiet room. "But it probably wasn't, was it?"

Clio took a deep breath and shook her head slowly. "I don't think so."

"What should we do?" Rebecca asked softly.

Clio closed the door. "I don't know, but whatever it is, we're going to need some help."

CHAPTER 8

LATER THAT EVENING, Rebecca and Clio found themselves sitting in twin bamboo chairs across from Kawanna at the large, ancient wooden desk in the office at the back of the costume shop. Rebecca was still thinking about the uneasy car ride home with Mr. Dunmore. When Rebecca had tried to tell Mr. Dunmore about Kyle's teeth, he hadn't said a word in response; it was almost as if he hadn't heard her.

The office was a windowless room, but it felt surprisingly warm and welcoming. The red-orange walls glowed like a sunset, reflected across the mirrors and framed movie posters dotting the walls. A sagging, peacock-blue velvet love seat nestled invitingly against the wall behind them, and a worn leather armchair and antique coffee table completed the cozy little seating area.

Kawanna's desk filled the rest of the room. Its massive mahogany legs were carved to look like lions, and the Tiffany lamp on its surface was shaped like a twisted, snarling dragon. It contrasted sharply with the sleek, silver laptop perched precariously near the edge. Rebecca shifted in her chair and focused her attention on the woman across the table.

Sitting in her gilded desk chair and framed by the overstuffed bookshelf behind her, Clio's aunt looked regal in her gold-and-purple head wrap and black cashmere poncho. Rebecca eyed her nervously. *What if she doesn't believe us?* Then she noticed Kawanna's nails: bright purple with a pattern of black bats. *She has to believe us.*

Rebecca poured out her story, with Clio chiming in. Kawanna's eyes widened with each new detail, and she gasped in surprise when Clio held up her injured hand.

When both girls had finally run out of breath, Kawanna turned to the bookshelf behind her, her voice full of wonder. "How can that be?" She rummaged through a teetering stack on one of the shelves.

"I know! There has to be an explanation, right?" Rebecca asked. "Something . . . you know, normal?"

Kawanna ran her fingers along the spines of the books, searching. "I don't know, honey. I've been reading ghost stories my whole life, but I never really believed they were true." She gestured at the shelf behind her. "But Clio and I have been sorting through some of these old books we found, and almost all of them are about unexplained events that happened right here in Piper. Events that sound a lot like what's happening with Kyle."

"What do you mean?" Rebecca asked.

"I mean that the lady who lived here before me also collected ghost stories, only I'm starting to think that the stories she collected may have been real."

"It's not just ghosts," Clio interjected. "There are all kinds of creatures in her books: vampires, shape-shifters, goblins, and stuff we don't even have a name for."

"*Lusus naturae,*" Kawanna added. "Creatures that are neither living nor dead. Monstrous hybrids that are shunned even in the Spirit World." She selected a few books from the shelf and piled them into a neat stack in the center of her desk.

"Lusus what? What are you talking about?" Rebecca turned from Clio to Kawanna, looking for some sign that the two were just teasing her, but both faces were deadly serious.

Kawanna slid the stack of books across the desk. "Think of all those boogeyman tales and movies where something goes after the children. Maybe there's a reason. What if they were real?"

"Is this some kind of joke?" Rebecca demanded. "Because if it is, it's not funny. My parents are doctors, remember? I know all those old ghost legends and spooky stories were made up before people had real explanations for why stuff happened."

Kawanna sat back in her chair and tented her fingers. "You're probably right," she said. "There has to be a more logical explanation. But what is it?"

Rebecca looked down, struggling to come up with something that made sense. She noticed a splotch of dried batter on her jeans and picked at it, remembering that just a few hours ago she had been rolling out icing in a busy, cheerful kitchen. It felt like weeks ago now. "I don't have one," she finally admitted.

"Neither do I," Clio said, "but we do know that there's something wrong with Kyle and his parents aren't able to see it." She looked from her aunt to Rebecca. "And if we're right, Kyle could be in real danger."

CHAPTER
9

EARLY THE NEXT morning, Rebecca pedaled back
to Kawanna's shop, her eyelids puffy and heavy.
She had been awake half the night going over the
events in her mind again and again, and when she
did finally nod off, her sleep was fitful and plagued
with nightmares. Snatches of images stayed with
her even after she woke: Kyle trapped in a cage of
sharp, pointed teeth. Her friends covered in moss,
their mouths stuffed with bright red leaves. Rebecca
standing powerless as they each disappeared, one
by one. Shortly before dawn she pulled the old

lady's books out of her backpack and opened them with a heavy sense of dread.

Once the sun had risen, Rebecca picked up her phone and sent a group text.

> Emergency meeting!
> Can U come 2 Kawanna's
> shop this AM?

Clio's reply came almost immediately.

> Already here.
> We have doughnuts!

A second later, a text came in from Tanya.

> Hope ur OK! C U soon!

Tanya and Clio woke up early, even on weekends, so Rebecca wasn't surprised that they had texted back so quickly. But a half hour later, Rebecca still hadn't heard back from Maggie. This wasn't unusual, since Maggie would sleep until noon if she had the chance. But Rebecca couldn't help wondering if maybe there was some other reason Maggie hadn't texted back.

Rebecca and Maggie had always butted heads. Back in second grade they had gotten into a screaming match in Maggie's front yard, and the whole neighborhood came out to see what was wrong. Within hours they were in Maggie's basement, setting up a hospital for their stuffed animals. Arguing was normal for them.

But lately, things with Maggie had been different. This wouldn't be the first time that Maggie hadn't returned Rebecca's texts, and they hardly ever hung out just the two of them anymore. Rebecca knew she could count on Tanya: good old, reliable Tanya who always got along with everybody. And Clio hadn't thought twice about helping yesterday, no matter how strange things had gotten. But could Rebecca still count on Maggie?

When Rebecca finished locking up her bike and walked inside the shop, Tanya and Clio were sprawled out on one of the Persian rugs, poring over a pile of wrinkled papers. Clio was writing down notes on a yellow legal pad, and Tanya was sketching some sort of diagram. On the counter behind them sat a white china platter piled high with a colorful assortment of pastries.

"Wow, when you said you had doughnuts, you weren't kidding," Rebecca said.

Clio looked up and laughed. "Yeah, my auntie doesn't mess around. When she does something, she tends to go all out."

Kawanna appeared from the back hallway carrying a celadon Japanese tea set on a silver tray. "It's true. I just can't help myself." She placed the tray on the counter and lifted the teapot by its bamboo handle, pouring tea into the small earthenware teacups. The fifth cup—Maggie's—remained empty. "Good morning, Rebecca."

"Good morning," Rebecca replied. "What are you guys working on?" She carefully extricated a blueberry-crumble doughnut from the pile and pushed aside a heap of rubber monster masks to sit on the floor next to her friends. Kawanna placed a steaming cup of tea next to her. Rebecca closed her eyes and inhaled the sweet jasmine scent. "Mmm, my favorite. Thanks, Kawanna."

"You have good taste," Kawanna replied. "It's my favorite, too." She placed her own teacup down gently and joined the group on the floor, curling her legs elegantly beneath her.

The girls sipped their tea, and Tanya held up a slim red book. "I have an idea, but it probably isn't going to make much sense. I don't know if it even makes sense to me!"

Rebecca read the title silently to herself: *Tales of the Night Queen*. "This is the book you were talking about the other day. Where does it fit in?"

Tanya placed the book in the center of their circle.

"I'm not sure yet," Tanya answered, "but what's happening to Kyle sounds an awful lot like one of the stories from this book." She opened the cover and pointed to an illustration near the front. It was a sketch of a tall woman with an elaborate silver crown, surrounded by shadowy spirits, zombie-like figures, and misshapen creatures that looked like a bizarre mix of humans and animals.

"This is the Night Queen. She rules some kind of place called the Nightmare Realm. I still don't know exactly where that is, but it sounds pretty terrifying. It's described as full of darkness and decay, with a bunch of shadow creatures and undead monsters wandering around, making people disappear. The book has a ton of stories and accounts of the Night Queen taking children, only nobody knows the kids are missing at first."

Rebecca put down her tea and picked up the book. "But why wouldn't they know?"

"In a lot of the stories, the Night Queen replaces the child with something called a changeling," Clio said. "You can find changeling stories all over the world. My auntie and I actually read a ton of them while we were with my parents in Europe a few years ago. It's an imposter that looks like the child, but it doesn't do a very good job of acting like one."

"But that doesn't make sense. Wouldn't the parents notice?" Rebecca asked.

"Well, think about the Dunmores," Clio responded. "You tried to tell them about the bite and Kyle's teeth, but they didn't even seem to hear you. Didn't you find that strange?"

"Everything about this is strange," Rebecca said. She turned to Tanya. "But I thought you didn't believe in supernatural stuff."

Tanya smiled. "I don't, normally, but then I thought about that Sherlock Holmes quote: 'When you have eliminated the impossible, whatever remains, however improbable, must be the truth.' It's definitely improbable, but right now it's the best explanation we have."

Kawanna chuckled. "I can't argue with that."

"But how can we be sure that's what's really going on?" Rebecca persisted.

"You know me," Tanya said. "Supernatural isn't really in my vocabulary, but science is. Now that we have our hypothesis, it's time for the next step of the scientific method: conducting our experiment."

"An experiment?" Rebecca asked. *Just like Tanya to make the impossible seem logical.*

"Well, it's more like a test," Tanya said. She lifted up a yellowed piece of paper and laid it carefully in the center of the carpet. Rebecca could see several precise drawings on the page, along with fading cursive handwriting. "Whenever the Night Queen replaces a child with a changeling, she leaves something of her own behind, hidden somewhere in the child's room. In the book they call it the Queen's Mark. If there's one in the Dunmores' house, it will give us clues about what to do next. If it's there," Tanya continued, looking around at the others, "it means the Night Queen took Kyle."

"She took him? As in *kidnapped?*" Rebecca couldn't breathe. The room was quiet for a moment.

Kawanna squeezed Rebecca's shoulder. "We don't know for sure that's what happened yet, honey. We just have to take this one step at a time. For right now, let's concentrate on finding the Mark."

Rebecca wiped at her eyes and picked up the paper. She took a deep breath. "Okay, so . . . the Queen's Mark. It says here it could be jewelry, feathers, bones, or even some of her hair. How will we know it belongs to her?"

"You know Kyle's house better than anyone," Tanya said. "Do you think you could find it without the family knowing?"

"Maybe," Rebecca said, "but if that's not really Kyle, I don't want to babysit there alone again."

"You may not have to," Kawanna said. "Is there a way you could drop by this morning, say you think you forgot something at the house last night?"

Rebecca pulled her phone out of her pocket. "I can give it a try."

Clio picked up her pad and clicked open her pen. "Let's get to work."

· · · · ·

A short time later, Rebecca and Tanya stood at the bottom of the steps leading up to the Dunmores' front porch. "I don't know why I'm so nervous," Rebecca whispered.

"We'll be fine," Tanya replied. "Nothing has changed since the last time you were here. If he isn't Kyle now, he wasn't Kyle then, either."

"Yeah, but it's different now. Now I *know*. What

if I act all awkward and everyone notices? What if I blow our cover?"

Tanya grinned and squeezed Rebecca's shoulder. "Relax; you're a babysitter, not a spy."

"I know. I just can't believe that any of this is really happening."

"Neither can I." Tanya grabbed her friend's hand and pulled her up the steps. "Scientifically speaking, it's totally new territory. I mean, this could change everything we think we understand about the universe. . . ." Tanya saw the look on Rebecca's face and trailed off. "Sorry."

Rebecca tried to smile. "It's okay. I just don't want to let anyone down, you know? Especially not Kyle."

"Rebecca, I've known you since we were four. Trust me; you're not going to let anyone down." Tanya rang the doorbell.

A disheveled Mrs. Dunmore opened the door. She was still in her robe and pajamas, her hair tangled. She held a cup of coffee in her hand. Behind her, Kyle scowled in his playpen, his toys scattered all over the floor. He looked pale and drawn, and there were dark circles under his eyes. "Hi, girls. We're having a bit of a slow start today, as you can see," Mrs. Dunmore said. She sighed and ran her hand over her eyes. "Rough morning around here." She took a long sip of her coffee. "You said you left something in Kyle's room? We didn't find anything, but you're welcome to look again."

"Thanks," Rebecca said. "It's for a project we're working on for school, and it's due really soon. Like, tomorrow, probably, or maybe Tuesday. It's a really, really important project, so, you know, obviously I have to find that . . . thing . . . I left."

Tanya nudged her inside the house. "Thanks, Mrs. Dunmore. We won't be long."

The girls walked up the stairs. Tanya lowered her voice. "Okay, I kind of get why you were nervous about blowing our cover."

Rebecca looked behind her. "Why? Was that bad? Do you think she could tell I was lying?"

"No!" Tanya said too quickly. "Great job. Just,

um, you know, maybe let me do the talking when we leave?"

From the doorway of Kyle's room, Rebecca could smell the same pungent, earthy scent from her last visit. And the handprints were back. All along the wall near the crib. Even on the ceiling, leading to the window—where scratch marks marred the sill. Deep ones.

"Wow. That's not creepy at all." Tanya pulled a digital camera out of her backpack and took some photos of the prints and scratches.

Rebecca opened the dresser drawers and carefully went through the piles of clothes. She unballed each pair of Kyle's tiny socks and looked inside before folding them up again and putting them back into the drawer.

"Find anything?" Tanya asked.

"Not yet," Rebecca answered. She lifted Kyle's favorite lamp; it was shaped like a sheep. She felt along the inside of the shade for a telltale bump, but the inside was smooth.

Tanya pulled the changing table away from the

wall and searched behind it. Rebecca ran her hand along the underside of the table, eyes unfocused out the window. Rebecca stood up sharply. Had something moved in the trees below?

There was a creak at the bottom of the stairs. "Do you girls need any help up there?"

"We're almost done. Thanks, Mrs. Dunmore," Tanya called. She turned back to Rebecca. "We should hurry," she whispered.

Rebecca turned away from the window and got on her hands and knees to study the crib. From down the hall, she could hear the sound of the Dunmores' bedroom door opening. She slipped her hand under the fitted sheet and ran her fingers across the mattress. "It's got to be over here," she whispered.

Tanya rushed to help. The floor creaked outside the Dunmores' room.

Someone was coming to check on them.

The footsteps outside the room grew closer, and Rebecca frantically felt behind the crib rails near the wall. Something soft and silky brushed her hand. Heart pounding, she pulled out a long, brown-and-gray-striped feather. Her arm shook slightly as she held it up. "Is this what I think it is?" she whispered.

Tanya unzipped her backpack and held out her hand. "Quick!" Rebecca handed her the feather, and Tanya dropped it in her bag just as Mr. Dunmore appeared in the doorway in faded gray sweats.

"Oh! I didn't know you were in here," he said.

Tanya held up a notebook from her backpack. "Yeah, Mrs. Dunmore let us in. Rebecca left this here, and we needed it for school."

"Well, I'm glad you found it. Do you girls want some breakfast?"

Rebecca felt her phone buzz in her pocket. "No thanks. We've got to get going." She stood up and followed Mr. Dunmore to the stairs, Tanya close behind her.

Mr. Dunmore paused at the front door. "Are you all right, Rebecca? You look pale."

"Oh, yeah, no, I'm . . . um . . . just . . . so . . . ," Rebecca stammered.

". . . so busy," Tanya finished. "We're so busy

working on this project, and we're worried we won't finish in time. So we really need to bounce."

"Thank you so much, Mr. Dunmore. See you soon." Rebecca gave a hurried wave and rushed down the steps. After the front door closed, she pulled out her phone. There was a text from Clio.

> Come 2 the shop as soon
> as U find something.
> We have a major problem.

As they hurried to their bikes, Rebecca glanced back at the house. The curtain in Kyle's window twitched. Someone—or something—was watching them ride away.

CHAPTER 10

"*WHAT DO YOU* mean, Kawanna can't come with us?" Rebecca demanded. She pointed to the pile of open books and papers piled on Kawanna's desk, the latter covered in Kawanna's spidery scrawl. "How are we going to get Kyle back without her?"

"Don't worry, honey," Kawanna said. "I may not be able to come with you, but I'll be here to help with every step of the planning." She held up a wizened leather-bound book whose pages were brown with age and mildew. "Clio and I found this while you were gone. It's the best information we have right now, and it says that only children themselves can challenge the Night Queen. Adults can't. Mainly because we can't see her."

Clio nodded in agreement. "Like Kyle's parents. We don't know exactly why yet, but the book says it's rare for any adult to see creatures from the Nightmare Realm clearly."

"I've been wondering about that," Tanya said. "And I have a theory. You know all those stories about babies waving to someone who isn't there? Or toddlers talking about their imaginary friends? Maybe the younger you are, the more you can see."

"So all those imaginary friends might actually be ghosts, or . . . something worse?" Rebecca shuddered, remembering her brother's imaginary friend, Bartleby. "Oh, that gives me the creeps."

"Yeah, that's super creepy," Clio agreed. "And it means that it's basically up to us to get Kyle back. But we have to find him first."

Rebecca straightened her shoulders. She would never leave Kyle to the Nightmare Realm. "So how do we do that?" she asked.

"Let's start by taking a look at that feather," Kawanna suggested. Rebecca handed it to her, and

Kawanna frowned as she ran her fingers down the shaft, noting the soft-fringed edges. She turned to the bookshelf behind her and pulled out a thick volume with a tattered gray dust jacket. "These edges tell me it's from some kind of owl," Kawanna said, pointing to the fluffy side of the feather. "Owls are night hunters. These fringes are what allow them to fly silently and surprise their prey; no other bird has them." She laid the feather on the desk and turned to the index at the back of the book. "The question is, which owl?"

"Why do we need to know which owl it is?" Rebecca asked.

Kawanna pointed to a page in the book and read, "*Although the queen loves all night hunters, there is only one bird whose feathers she considers regal enough to wear as her mantle: the great horned owl.*" She looked up. "And that's exactly who this feather belongs to."

"The Queen's Mark," Rebecca whispered. She stared at the feather. *This is real. This is all real. Kyle is missing.*

"The next step is to get the changeling to show

its true form," Clio said. "Once it does, it returns to the creature who created it . . ."

". . . giving us a road map right to the Nightmare Realm," Tanya finished.

"Exactly," Clio said. "Now, a changeling can be all kinds of things: a rotten log, a bundle of sticks, or even a spirit in disguise. There are lots of ways you can see the true form. In Germany, they recommended hitting or whipping it, or trying to burn it in the oven."

"What?!" Rebecca screeched, horrified.

Kawanna chuckled and patted Rebecca's arm reassuringly. "Don't worry. We're not going to be listening to the Germans."

"Actually, most places mentioned beating or burning," Clio admitted, "but that's obviously not happening. We knew there had to be some other way. And we found one!" Her hazel eyes sparkled with excitement.

"What is it?" Rebecca asked.

Kawanna raised a finger in the air. "Wait," she said to her niece. "Don't tell them right away. Give them a chance to guess. With a riddle."

"A riddle?" Rebecca asked, confused.

"The Night Queen loves riddles," Clio explained, "and so does my auntie. Whenever our family was traveling, she was forever making up riddles for, like, the simplest things: 'What can you catch, but not throw? A cold.' Stuff like that."

"I had to do something to keep you busy on all those airplanes and trains. You were a fussy little thing!" Kawanna said. She folded her arms. "This is an especially good riddle for you, Rebecca: What needs to be broken before it can be used?"

Rebecca thought carefully. Why would this be a good riddle for her? What was something that she broke in order to use it? The other three looked at her expectantly, encouraging looks on their faces. She pictured Kyle, alone and scared, without even his teddy bear to comfort him. Her mind went completely blank. "I can't . . . I don't know. A . . . branch?" she asked lamely.

"Wait, I think I've got it," Tanya said. "I'll give you a hint. Think about baking."

Rebecca turned her mind back to the riddle and tried to relax. After a moment, she spoke. "Oh, is it an egg? You have to break the shell before you can use it."

"Yes! It's an egg!" Clio cheered. "Believe it or not, almost every story we read mentioned using eggs to reveal a changeling's true form."

"But how?" Rebecca asked. "Do we have to break them over the changeling or something?"

"It's actually a little bit weirder than that—this is where you come in. Changeling-Kyle has to actually see us cook something inside the eggshell, and then we have to give it to him," Clio said.

"That's so random," Rebecca said. "Why eggs?"

Clio shrugged. "The websites I found said that cooking inside an egg was considered such an odd thing to do that it would shock the changeling into forgetting that it was pretending to be a baby. But whatever it is, something about it freaks them out enough to turn them back."

"We were thinking maybe you could figure out how to make cupcakes with the eggshells as the cupcake tins," Kawanna said.

"Well, I definitely like it better than that German plan." Rebecca thought for a moment. "I think I could probably do it, but I'll need to practice first."

"I'll put together a grocery list," Kawanna said, standing up. She carefully smoothed the indigo tunic she wore over skull-patterned black leggings and adjusted the gauzy scarf around her neck before disappearing into the back of the shop.

"While you're practicing, Tanya and I will continue to research the queen," Clio said.

"What do we do when we find her? How do we get Kyle back safely?" Rebecca asked.

"It's hard to say. Every creature is different, and all we found about fighting them so far is just in a bunch of old poems and songs," Tanya said.

Clio smoothed out a curled scroll and squinted at the elaborate calligraphy. "It's a lot of stuff like this: '*Cruelty is as cruelty does, but none can rule the heart that loves.*' Whatever that means. Or how about, '*Bend the willow, bend the rod, with iron shoes the Queene be shod.*' Is that supposed to be a good thing or a bad thing?"

Tanya ran her fingers through her short-cropped hair. "They're all like that. This is a scientist's worst nightmare. Why can't there be a nice, simple text-book or some kind of how-to guide?"

"So basically all we know so far is that we have to bake a cake in an egg and be ready to talk like Shakespeare?" Rebecca gnawed anxiously at her thumbnail. "I guess there's still time to figure out something better, right?"

Outside, a gust of wind sent dead leaves skittering across the sidewalk. A bright maple leaf flew up and pressed against the glass door, its edges flapping.

"Maybe not. I think we need to be ready to move by next Saturday. That's the date of the next full moon," Clio said. "It's one of the only times the gateway opens between our world and the Nightmare Realm. The Night Queen took Kyle during the last one."

Rebecca remembered the silvery glow of the full moon falling across Kyle's bedroom the night of the storm.

"Next Saturday is the Harvest Ball Fund-Raiser for the hospital. Mrs. Dunmore is on the board. She asked me to babysit," Rebecca said. The leaf dropped to the sidewalk again before another gust came along, and it danced away down the street.

"Good," Tanya said. "That means they'll be out until at least midnight. Do you think that will give us enough time?"

"Let's hope so," Clio said, "because it may be the only chance we have."

CHAPTER 11

THE KITCHEN WAS a mess. Broken eggshells littered Kawanna's shiny zinc countertops, and stray drops of egg yolk dotted the black-and-white tile floor. The kitchen table was dusted with a thick layer of flour, and a pile of dirty baking pans teetered precariously on the yellow vintage stove.

Rebecca's first challenge had been just figuring out how to make a baking cup out of an eggshell. She had lost count of how many eggs cracked open in her hands before she finally searched the internet and found a YouTube video helpfully entitled

"Cutting the Top Off an Egg." Then, on her first batch of cupcakes, the eggshell cups had tipped over during baking, spilling the batter and scorching the bottom of the pan. For her second batch, she figured out a way to line an egg carton with foil and stand the eggshells up so they wouldn't tip over. This felt like a huge victory until she took the cupcakes out of the oven and discovered that the overfilled shells had exploded from the pressure of the expanded batter. It was on her third batch that she had found the right mix of batter and balance and made something even resembling an edible cupcake.

Rebecca put her hands on her hips and surveyed the damage. "I'm so sorry, Kawanna. I promise I'm not normally this messy when I cook. Baking in eggshells is a lot harder than I thought."

"Better you than me." Kawanna laughed. "Clio can tell you that I've never been much of a cook. We have a deal whenever her parents go away: I do all the shopping and cleaning, and Clio does all the cooking."

"That sounds fun," Rebecca said.

"It's worked for us so far. Clio makes a pretty mean stir-fry."

Rebecca picked up a stack of muffin tins and baking pans and set them on the counter next to the sink. She squirted dish soap on a yellow sponge and started scrubbing.

Kawanna stood up. "You wash; I'll dry. Then in a little while, we'll switch." She grabbed a dish towel and took the dripping pan from Rebecca's hands. "Do you and your parents ever bake together?"

"Not really." Rebecca shrugged. "They're not good in the kitchen. I mean, my dad cooks sometimes on the weekends, and my mom makes a big spread at Passover, but other than that, it's mostly take-out and microwave dinners." She handed another pan to Kawanna. "They're pretty tired after work."

"I don't blame them," Kawanna said. "The older you get, the longer the days feel." She took the stack of dry, clean pans and put them back in the drawer under the stove. "I hope that at least they enjoy eating your culinary creations, even if they don't help make them."

Rebecca laughed. "They definitely like eating them! They let me take all the baking classes I want, and they've helped me buy some of the equipment my babysitting money doesn't cover, like a stand mixer."

"So what gave you the baking bug in the first place?" Kawanna asked, picking up a muffin tin.

"I have my Nai Nai to thank for that," Rebecca explained. "She was my dad's mom. She used to live with us when I was little, and she could make anything! She's the one who taught mc to bake, but shc died when I was nine."

Kawanna's face softened. "You must miss her."

Rebecca smiled sadly. "Nai Nai was so much fun. She was obsessed with basketball, and she was always yelling at the TV and cursing out the players in Cantonese. She spoke Mandarin, too, but she said that Cantonese was better for cursing. My dad would always try to cover my ears!"

Kawanna grinned. "She sounds like my kind of lady." She took Rebecca's place washing at the sink and glanced at the clock. "I thought the girls would be back by now. What could be taking them so long?"

Rebecca dried a bright-green mixing bowl and put it back in the cabinet. "I know they were going to stop by Maggie's house after they hit the library, so maybe they're still over there." Rebecca pictured the bike path to the library. Part of it skirted the woods near Kyle's house, didn't it? She looked outside at the waning light and the lengthening shadows between the buildings across the street. She pulled out her phone. "I'll send them a quick text to check in."

Where R U?

Kawanna put a handful of freshly washed spoons on the counter and reached under the sink for a new sponge. "I was surprised Maggie wasn't at the shop this morning."

Rebecca shrugged and picked up a spoon, drying it slowly. "Yeah, Maggie's kind of a heavy sleeper." She checked her phone. No new texts. "Huh. Why aren't they answering?"

Kawanna wiped down the counters, scraping at the burned egg with the rough side of the sponge. She walked to the kitchen doorway and peeked into the hall. "I'll go check the shop. Maybe they're up front and we didn't hear them come in." She disappeared down the hall.

Rebecca looked at her phone again. Nothing. She texted again.

> Hello?????

Outside, the wrought iron streetlights were just starting to wink on, bathing the pavement below in pools of yellow light. A few crows perched on a power line burst into a flurry of flight, their shrieking caws fading away toward the woods. Her phone sat silent on the countertop.

In the twilight outside, a heavy shadow swooped onto the roof across the street. It fluffed its feathers, settling into stillness. An owl.

Kawanna came back into the room with her phone. "Not there. I'll call Clio. You try Tanya and Maggie."

Rebecca called Tanya and listened to the phone ring. And ring. Why wasn't Tanya picking up? Rebecca hung up and tried Maggie. The call went straight to voice mail. "Any luck?"

Kawanna shook her head. "No answer."

Rebecca looked out the window again. The owl was gone.

Just then, they heard the jingling of the chimes on the shop's front door.

"Sorry we're late," Clio called, "but we brought reinforcements!" Three sets of footsteps trooped down the long hallway that led to Kawanna's tiny apartment behind the shop.

"Where were you? Why didn't you answer my texts?" Rebecca asked. "We were so worried!"

"Oh, relax, Rebecca. We're barely even late!" Maggie said.

"It's already dark outside, and none of you were answering your phone, and there's an evil Night Queen out there! What are we supposed to think?!" Rebecca said, annoyed at how cheerful and carefree they all seemed.

"We're really sorry. Maggie took forever to get

ready, and then at the library her phone kept going off, so the librarian made us all put our phones on Do Not Disturb. I guess we just forgot to switch them back on again." Tanya sniffed the air. "Something smells good! Rebecca must have been working her magic!"

Rebecca tried to smile. "Yeah, it took a few tries, but I think we've got it. Kawanna was a great sous-chef."

"Oh, I can't take any credit. It was all Rebecca," Kawanna said.

Maggie shoved her hands in her pockets and yawned. "I can't believe you're all actually doing this," she said. "I mean, do you really believe this stuff?"

"Hey, none of us really knows what to believe, but we don't exactly have a choice," Tanya said.

"I guess, but I don't know how Rebecca's egg-cakes are going to do anything." Maggie laughed.

"Well, maybe not, but at least they look cool." Rebecca held up a brown eggshell, picked at the cutoff top, and carefully peeled back the shell. In her hand sat a perfect egg-shaped cake.

"Isn't that something?" Kawanna murmured, shaking her head and smiling.

"Who wants a taste?" Rebecca asked, and Clio and Tanya crowded around the table. Maggie hung back. Rebecca handed eggs around to everyone.

Kawanna held her egg in the air. "Let's have a toast!" she said grandly.

"To exploration!" Tanya called.

"And research!" Clio added.

"And teamwork!" Rebecca cried.

The group tapped the eggs together, cracking them, and eagerly began peeling off the shells to reveal the golden cake within.

Only Rebecca seemed to notice that Maggie hadn't joined in the toast.

CHAPTER 12

A SHORT TIME later, the four girls sat around a pile of books and papers on the black lacquer coffee table in Kawanna's office. Rebecca could hear the sounds of Kawanna moving around the shop in front, sliding hangers along racks and laying out trays of jewelry and beaded handbags on top of the counters. Rebecca had Kawanna's laptop open on the table in front of her, and Clio riffled through a stack of old books.

Tanya read back from a long list on the yellow legal pad. "Okay, so here's the list of what we have so far to keep Changeling-Kyle calm and happy while we try to change him back. Changelings like music, songs, dancing, nature stuff, and—apparently—letting him bite us. Or at least according to Clio."

"Trust me, he loves it. Laughs like a hyena. But it's someone else's turn to get bitten. My fingers can't take any more abuse!"

Maggie sat back in the leather easy chair and draped her leg over the arm, her pink jeweled flip-flop dangling from her big toe. She tapped at her phone, her eyes intent on the screen. "So say this thing works, and it turns out that Kyle is some kind of monster thing and not just a grumpy baby who's had a couple of bad days. What then? I mean, it's not like the monster is going to change back into Kyle, right? So what's the point?"

Rebecca leaned forward in disbelief. "Are you serious? The point is getting Kyle back!"

"Yeah, duh, I know that, Becks. I'm not stupid. But what is the cake thing going to even *do*? It just seems like a waste of time." Maggie rolled her eyes. "Actually, this whole thing seems like a waste of time, if you ask me," she mumbled under her breath.

Rebecca's voice rose and she stood up. *"A waste of time?!"*

Maggie dropped her phone in her lap, finally facing the other girls. "Yeah, a waste of time! I mean, seriously, you guys. We don't even know where the Nightmare Realm is, much less how to find it. And Clio told me about what the Night Queen can do, okay? She doesn't seem like someone to mess with. She could make us her prisoners, turn us into cockroaches, or even kill us! You get that, right? Like, our parents would never see us again."

"So are we supposed to just give up on him because it seems *hard?*"

"Not just hard, Becks. Impossible. I mean, if she's really that powerful, do you really think a few kids stand any chance of finding Kyle, much less getting him back from her? Are you delusional?"

"Hold on. Everybody just calm down," Tanya said. "This is obviously a stressful situation, and fighting will only make it worse."

Maggie snorted. "A math test is a stressful situation. This is, like, Zombie Apocalypse–level stuff."

"C'mon, Maggie, don't be so dramatic. It's not helping. Clio and I did a lot of research while Rebecca was working on the cake, and I think we actually have a pretty good plan."

"Wow. I'm really sure you guys are going to beat an all-powerful ghost queen with your *pretty good plan.*"

"Well, technically she's not a ghost queen," Clio said. "Although she does have some ghostlike qualities." Clio noticed Maggie's darkening expression. "You know what? It doesn't matter. The point is, I think the plan could work. And it all begins with Rebecca's cake."

Rebecca shrugged. "No pressure, right?" She giggled nervously and saw Maggie roll her eyes again.

Maggie crossed her arms. "So this critter takes a bite of Rebecca's magic cake or whatever, transforms into some freak thing, and then just books it into the woods back to Mama. Okay, fine. So how are you supposed to follow it? What if you lose it?"

"We thought of that, and I think I may have come up with a solution," Tanya said. "We know that changelings can be all kinds of things, but most of them are at least partly made up of something old and decaying, like dead leaves or something. I have to do some experiments at home, but if our changeling is rotten or has any kind of mold or fungus on it, I think I have a way to track it if we lose it in the chase."

"But we won't lose it," Rebecca said. "There's no way I'm going to let that happen."

"Looks like you have a foolproof plan, I guess," Maggie shot back sarcastically. "Until you meet the queen, that is."

"Until *we* meet the queen," Tanya said. "We need you there, too, Maggie."

"Isn't this Rebecca's deal? What do you need me for?"

Rebecca couldn't believe what she was hearing. "What is your problem with me? Seriously, what have I done?"

Tanya's voice rose almost to a shout. "I said not now, you guys! Enough! We need to focus here. Everybody has to do their part if we have any hope of succeeding."

"Agreed," Clio added. "Maggie's right; it's not an easy plan, but we worked so hard to put it together. Do you two really want it to fall apart just because you can't figure out how to get along?"

Rebecca exploded. "I'm trying to get along! In case anyone has forgotten, this is about saving a baby! A baby that I have been taking care of since he was tiny. First tooth, first words, and, just a few weeks ago, some of his first steps." She leaned toward Maggie, struggling to control her emotions. "Whatever your deal is with me, whatever I did, I'm sorry, okay? Tell me what it is, or don't tell me; I don't care. I just want to get Kyle back, all right? Just please, Maggie, can you think about something other than yourself?"

"You're calling me selfish?!" Maggie snapped. "Who exactly is being selfish here? Kyle disappeared on your watch, and now you expect all of us to drop everything and *risk our lives* to get him back because you weren't paying attention?"

Rebecca's vision swam. From the corner of her eye, she noticed Clio slipping out of the room and down the hall. "If that's what you think, then what are you even doing here? Since the moment Clio, Tanya, and I realized what was going on, we have spent every second working our tails off to come up with a way to save Kyle. And what, exactly, have you done so far? Shown up? And you needed a personal invitation to even do that!"

A loud metallic crash reverberated through the room, cutting through Rebecca's crackling anger. Clio stood in the doorway, holding a large brass gong in one hand and a mallet in the other. Her perfectly arched eyebrows were knitted together. "Did that finally get your attention? Good. Because I have just about lost patience with you two. Now you need to pull it together and pull it together fast, because we only have one shot at this. If we don't get Kyle back before the next full moon sets, the Night Queen gets to keep him forever."

CHAPTER 13

GIVEN THE LATE night the Dunmores had planned, it hadn't been too difficult to persuade them to let the four girls come over to watch Kyle together. But that had been just about the only thing that had gone smoothly in the days leading up to the Harvest Ball. Maggie had participated in the preparations only grudgingly, and Rebecca was too focused on Kyle to try to mend the growing rift. The memory of Clio's words echoed through her mind. *Forever.* The Night Queen will keep him *forever.* Her heart seized every time she imagined Kyle eternally trapped in a dark world, his parents never knowing what happened to him. Whatever was really bothering Maggie would have to wait, and in the meantime they avoided each other as much as possible.

That night at the Dunmores', four exhausted girls stood in a nervous circle around the changeling baby, who eyed them watchfully from his high chair.

Changeling-Kyle's teeth were sharper than ever, and his skin had a dull, sallow hue. His eyes, once bright blue, were now almost black and sunken into his gaunt face. His hands were curled into themselves like talons and covered with dark, downy hair. Although Rebecca knew that Kyle's parents wouldn't be able to see the changes, it was still hard to believe that they hadn't noticed anything amiss.

Rebecca could see that even Maggie was stunned by the transformation. Her green eyes were large with worry, and her cheeks, normally rosy and freckled, had blanched to a pasty white.

She turned to her friends in shock, her voice a terrified whisper. "Is he . . . is that how . . . ? He's so . . . horrible!"

Tanya grabbed Maggie's arm and squeezed it. "Not now. He'll hear you," she whispered, her lips barely moving.

Forcing a smile on her face, Rebecca bent down to look the changeling in the face. "Hey, sunshine. You remember Clio. . . ." The baby gave a wicked grin and snapped his jaws, and Clio took an involuntary step backward. "And Tanya and Maggie will be babysitting you today, too."

Tanya smiled. "Hi, cutie." She nudged Maggie, who still stood there dumbly. "Say hello, Maggie." Maggie shook her head, and Changeling-Kyle's face puckered with suspicion.

"I . . . I . . . can't. There's just no way. I'm not doing this." Maggie backed out of the room, tears in her terrified eyes. The baby's expression darkened, and he began to struggle in his high chair.

"Maggie, wait!" Tanya called after her.

"Let her go," Clio said. She turned back to the

baby. "How about some music?" She opened her mouth and began to sing:

> "O, don't you remember, a long time
>   ago,
> Those two little babies, their names I
>   don't know
> They were stolen away one bright
>   summer's day
> And left in a wood, so I've heard
>   folks say."

At the sound of the melody, Kyle's expression softened and he stopped struggling. Rebecca sidled over to Tanya. "What is she singing?" she whispered.

"It's an old folk song," Tanya whispered back. "We'll keep singing to calm him down while you go after Maggie."

"Me? You know she's not going to listen to me!"

"Look, you know we can't pull this off unless you two can work together. We don't have time to argue, okay? We've got to get Maggie back here."

Rebecca hurried out of the kitchen, dreading the confrontation to come. Confronting the Night Queen was terrifying, but at least it was something she understood: The Night Queen was wrong, and they were right. It was easy to know who had to win and why. But she had no idea how to sort things out with her friend. She felt like Maggie had been pretty awful, but it seemed like Maggie thought that Rebecca was the one who was wrong. *We don't have time for this right now!* Rebecca thought desperately as she ventured into the velvety shadow of the dining room.

"Maggie? Maggie, where are you?" she called, trying to smooth out the edge in her voice. She moved slowly through the living room, turning on a dim table lamp with a loud click. The room was devoid of life, but there in the center of the cream carpet was another bright red maple leaf. Rebecca shoved it into her pocket and moved into the front hall. She flipped the light switch, but nothing happened. Was Maggie still in the house?

She walked cautiously toward the coat closet. The door was slightly ajar. "Maggie?" Rebecca whispered, pushing open the door. It let out a long, low creak, making her skin crawl. Rebecca forced herself to shove her arms into the row of coats, pushing them aside. No Maggie.

As she crept up the stairs, she could hear Clio and Tanya singing in harmony.

> "Now the robins so red, how swiftly
>   they sped
> They put out their wide wings and over
>   them spread
> And all the day long on the branches
>   among
> They sweetly did whistle and this was
>   their song."

"Maggie!" Rebecca called again. The haunting lyrics set her already frayed nerves further on edge. Why wasn't Maggie answering? She heard the sound of ragged breathing and paused. It was coming from farther down the dark hallway. A huddled shape stood in the doorway to Kyle's room. As she drew closer, her nostrils filled with that heavy, damp smell of fungus and worms, of wood rotting from within. Her stomach twisted. Her hand reached cautiously forward and touched the huddled figure.

It turned with a bloodcurdling shriek, and Rebecca caught only a flash of red-rimmed green eyes and a blotchy, tearstained face before it struck her and she fell to the ground.

"Oh no! Rebecca! I didn't know that was you!" Maggie said breathlessly, crouching down next to her. "Are you all right?"

Rebecca took a deep breath. "I'm fine. Just had the wind knocked out of me." Sitting up, she reached for Maggie. "What happened? Why didn't you answer?"

Maggie shook her head. "I couldn't. I was . . . I mean . . . just look," she stammered, pointing into Kyle's room. It was flooded with the silvery light from the full moon outside, but the usual shapes of Kyle's furniture and toys seemed softened and distorted, as though they were covered in glittering sheets. Not sheets; moss. Everything in Kyle's room was covered in a layer of rich green, wet with dew. Tendrils of cobwebs hung from the ceiling like ancient gray burial shrouds. Bile-colored mold covered Kyle's mattress, and skeletal branches grew haphazardly from the rocking chair by the window. Patches of pale, poisonous-looking mushrooms sprung from the soggy carpet.

"What . . . what is that?" Maggie said, shaking.

"I don't know," Rebecca admitted, "but I think it means that we don't have much time. Come on! We have to get back downstairs." She grabbed Maggie's hand and pulled her toward the stairwell, but Maggie stopped her.

"I can't go back down there."

"Please, Maggie, we need you!"

Her back against the wall, Maggie slid to the floor and hugged her knees. Tears choked her voice. "Look, I just can't, okay? I'm not like you. Ever since we were little, I've been hearing about what a 'good influence' you are. Like I'm so lucky to have you around, because otherwise I'd be a total wreck. Well, look, here we are and, guess what, I'm a disaster. I mean, we're talking about a kidnapped baby, and some kind of, of . . . creature downstairs.

This is serious, adult stuff. It's a *missing baby*, Becks. I can't fix this! I can't even keep track of my own lunch box."

From downstairs Rebecca could hear Kyle growing restless with the girls' singing. His fists pounded on the tray of his high chair. Rebecca needed to get back to the kitchen. And fast. But they needed Maggie's help in order to save Kyle. "Look, Mags, I know how you feel."

Maggie's eyes flashed with anger. "No, you don't!"

Rebecca's voice rose. "Okay, yeah, I get it. I'm not you. And it's true I do a lot of stuff on my own."

Maggie sighed impatiently. "I know! You don't need to tell me again!"

"Let me finish, okay? I'm not some special person who's just naturally responsible. I'm responsible because I *had* to be. My parents work all the time, and when Nai Nai died, they still had to work, so I had to figure out how to do stuff on my own. I would give anything to have Nai Nai back again; not just because I loved her, but because I miss having someone else help me with the hard stuff when my parents aren't around."

Maggie's voice got quiet. "I'm sorry. I know you still miss her a lot."

"But even in my hardest times without Nai Nai, I've always known that if I *really* needed to, I could pick up the phone and Mom and Dad would come rushing home from work and help me. So I wanted to prove to myself and to them that they could count on me, just like I can count on them."

Rebecca grabbed Maggie's arm. "But this time I can't count on them. I can't even *tell* them about this. There is no way they would ever believe me. We're talking about magic and creatures—stuff I didn't even believe in until a few days ago! There is a very real baby who is in very real, grown-up danger, but grown-ups cannot save him. I don't know how to rescue a kidnapped baby. I don't even know how to find him! But I do know that we're the only ones who can. We are Kyle's only chance."

"I get that, but what am I gonna do? At least

you guys did research and made a plan. You've all got it together. If I go back down there, knowing me, I'd probably just mess everything up." Maggie picked at her shoelace.

Rebecca bent her head so that she was looking into Maggie's eyes. "Remember when we both got the flu in second grade and Carolyn Hanson started calling me Barf Girl after I threw up on my math book? She and all her friends followed me around every recess for a week, making fun of me until I cried."

"Ugh, Carolyn was the worst."

"Yeah, she was awful. But you stopped her, remember? You were still sick, but you made your mom let you come to school anyway, and that day at recess you told them off so hard, they were all in tears when you walked away. They never bothered me again. You stand up for people, and you don't care what the consequences are; you just do what's right. You were totally fearless that day. And you made me feel braver, too. You still do."

A loud, long wail rent the air, and Clio's and Tanya's voices stopped abruptly. Rebecca stood up and leaned down, offering her hand to Maggie. "Please, Mags. We have to get down there, and I am so scared. I can't do this without you."

Maggie reached up and squeezed Rebecca's hand. "So you promise you have no idea what you're doing, then, either?"

Rebecca pulled her friend to her feet. "I promise I have no idea what I'm doing. Let's go."

CHAPTER 14

THEY RETURNED TO chaos. Changeling-Kyle's waxy face had turned a deep red, and his screams filled the kitchen. He wouldn't even look at Tanya, who was trying to entice him to play with some twigs and leaves she had gathered from outside. A teething ring lay on the floor near his high chair, and Clio was nursing another bite on her hand. "You'd think I would have learned by now," she mumbled.

Rebecca rushed over and clapped her hands to get the baby's attention. "Hi, Kyle-bear. Are you hungry?" At the word *hungry*, his eyes lit up. A forked tongue snaked out and licked eagerly at his leathery lips. Rebecca fought the urge to gag. "I thought so! We're going to make a yummy special cupcake just for you."

Maggie and Tanya quickly began unloading the supplies from Rebecca's bag while Clio rummaged through the first aid kit and found something for her hand. Rebecca began to sing as she turned on the oven to preheat it, her ragged voice barely rising above the sound of their nervous preparations.

> *"Hot cross buns*
> *Hot cross buns*
> *One a penny, two a penny*
> *Hot cross buns."*

To save time, Rebecca had mixed the batter at home and stored it in a Tupperware bowl. All she had to do now was prepare the eggs. Kyle watched her intently as she took off the lid and stirred the batter with a wooden spoon. Behind her, Maggie and Tanya carefully removed the eggs from an egg carton and joined in her song. Clio, her hand clean and bandaged, took over the stirring from Rebecca.

Now came the difficult part. While Maggie and Tanya lined the empty carton with foil, Rebecca picked up the first egg and, with hands shaking, used the tip of a small paring knife to gently scratch a circle around the top. Once she had etched the circle completely, she pushed the knife tip into the crack she had made. In her anxiety, she pushed the knife tip too hard and the egg collapsed, shattering into a dozen pieces and soaking her hands with yolk. Kyle squealed with delight. "Well, at least you're not screaming," Rebecca said to him, and the other girls laughed nervously.

Rinsing her hands, Rebecca took a deep breath. She tried to think only of what she had to do next: cut the eggs. But she couldn't help worrying about what would happen after that. What would Changeling-Kyle turn into? Would it hurt them? And even worse, what if they were wrong, and this *was* the real Kyle? What if he stayed like this forever?

Relax. She closed her eyes. *Focus.*

Rebecca remembered standing in her own kitchen with Nai Nai at her side, sunlight streaming through the window above the sink. Every fall, Rebecca used to help Nai Nai make mooncakes, and Nai Nai would guide her as she measured out the precise mix of kansui, golden syrup, oil, and cake flour to make the dough turn a perfect golden yellow. That last year when Nai Nai was sick, she had sat on a kitchen chair with a fuzzy, hand-knit hat covering her bald head and watched as Rebecca went through each step, chiming in when she was needed. "Just a pinch of salt in the egg yolk."

Rebecca remembered the pride she had felt when her beautiful mooncakes came out of the oven. Nai Nai had beamed when she took her first bite. "*Hen hao.* Perfect!"

Rebecca picked up the second egg, picturing Nai Nai standing beside her. Again she carefully etched a circle around the top of the egg with her paring knife. Then, slowly and carefully, she burrowed the tip of the knife into the crack she had carved in the egg. Gently, she wiggled the tip back and forth until it slipped under the shell, and she popped the top off the egg. Rebecca let out the breath she had been holding. She emptied the egg into a small bowl and rinsed the shell carefully in the sink. Kyle's dark eyes brimmed with curiosity.

"Watch this, Kyle," Rebecca said. She spooned a small amount of batter into the egg and then nestled it into the carton. Kyle gaped and squirmed with confused excitement. "Now we're going to bake it." Rebecca put the carton onto a metal baking sheet and slid it into the oven. He shrieked and began rocking wildly in his high chair.

"Easy, easy!" Maggie cried, and she rushed to grab the high chair before it tipped over. Kyle's hairy hands flailed wildly.

Clio looked down at the timer on her phone. "We just have to keep him entertained for seven more minutes," she said tensely.

"And then what?" Tanya asked as she slipped a teething ring onto his high chair tray, keeping well out of reach of Kyle's snapping jaws.

"Then I guess we'll find out if your experiment worked," Rebecca answered. "But in the meantime, we can try this." She reached into her bag and pulled out a brown plastic recorder.

"A recorder? Seriously? Is this third-grade music class?" Maggie asked.

Rebecca's cheeks turned a deep scarlet. "It's all I could find. And Maggie, you're going to have to play it. You know I don't have a musical bone in my body." She passed the instrument into Maggie's open hand.

"It's true," Maggie said. "You are the most terrible musician I have ever heard. I didn't even think it was possible to play a recorder out of tune, but somehow you managed it."

"Is she really that bad?" Clio whispered to Tanya.

Tanya nodded and leaned in closer to Clio. "Our music teacher made Rebecca lip-synch during the recorder concert. Have you ever heard of anyone lip-synching on a recorder?"

Clio's jaw dropped, and a bark of surprised laughter left her mouth.

Kyle let out a low, animal whine and clawed at his high chair tray. "Hurry up, Mags! It's all about you right now," Rebecca said.

"Yeah, because who doesn't want to impress a

baby-monster, right?" Maggie said with a nervous grin. Kyle's wriggling grew more violent.

"Maggie!" Rebecca said impatiently.

"Okay, okay . . . take it easy! I got this," Maggie answered, and put the recorder to her lips. Kyle and the girls grew quiet. She closed her eyes, and the lilting opening strains of "Stairway to Heaven" filled the anticipatory silence of the room.

"Really, Mags? Led Zeppelin?" Tanya whispered.

"It's all I can remember how to play!" Maggie hissed, and returned to her playing.

Tanya smirked and turned to Clio. "Our music teacher was really into classic rock," she explained.

"Whatever it is, I think it's working," Clio said softly, pointing at Kyle. His sunken eyes closed sleepily, and his wiry limbs relaxed. Clio checked the timer. "Maggie, you just need to keep playing for about five more minutes."

"That won't be a problem," Tanya whispered. "The song is, like, eight minutes long. Half the audience fell asleep during the third-grade concert."

Rebecca clicked on the oven light and bent forward, peering through the window to check the egg-cake. "It's almost ready," she called softly, and felt her neck and shoulders relax. For this moment, at least, everything was under control.

"That actually sounds really good," Clio said. Maggie shrugged, and her lips curved into a smile around the recorder's mouthpiece. Kyle's breathing deepened, and the room fell into a relaxed hush.

When Clio's timer went off, Kyle screamed. Forgetting herself, Rebecca threw open the oven door and reached for the hot pan, burning her fingers. "Ouch!" she hissed, and Kyle let out a guttural growl of pleasure.

Tanya tossed her a pair of oven mitts. Rebecca pulled out the pan and turned off the oven, peeking in the eggshell to find the cake cooked a perfect golden brown. Rebecca looked at the other girls. "It's ready."

Maggie moved closer to the back door, checking to make sure it was unlocked. Tanya slung a small pack on her back. Clio bent to tighten the laces on her running shoes and headed to the front door. Rebecca looked at everyone. "Everybody good?" she asked.

"I think we're as ready as we can be," Clio answered, and the other girls gave short nods.

"Here we go," Rebecca said under her breath. She turned to Kyle. "Look, Kyle! Here's your special cupcake just for you." She tapped the egg cake on the counter and gently started to peel the shell off, holding it up to show Kyle what she was doing. Slowly and gently, she placed the cake on the high chair tray in front of him.

The baby's eyes widened and grew darker, until even the whites had turned jet-black. His wan face flushed between a jaundiced yellow and a muddy maroon, and the veins of his high forehead bulged dangerously.

"What's happening?" Clio called from the front hall.

"I think he's changing!" Tanya shouted. "Be ready!"

Rebecca gaped in horror as Kyle's limbs snapped and stretched into thin, sinewy branches knotted with bulging pustules of fungus. His gnarled fingers lengthened into long, pale mushrooms, spores falling from them like rotten snow. Scales spread across his feet, the toes bending into long, sharp talons. Mildew grew on the pale blue onesie he wore, and it tore open, revealing a body of rotting wood.

Rebecca felt the bile rising in her throat. Every part of her wanted to run screaming from the house and get as far away as possible from the monster in front of her. The very idea that she had kissed and cuddled this putrid creature was almost more than she could bear. It was only the image of Kyle—the *real* Kyle—somewhere in the woods that kept her feet rooted and her eyes on the face of the imposter that had taken his place.

The changeling's face caved like a rotted apple, the black, sunken eyes retreating deeper to form empty hollows in the creature's pitted face. Cup-shaped fungus sprouted where the ears had been, and the sharp teeth grew more jagged. The dark maw of the mouth opened, and a high, feral whine rent the air.

Its ropy arms tore at the high chair, flinging the tray to the floor, and it leaped across the room in a puff of foul-smelling powder. Drips of slime

streaked the counter as it shot past, knocking Rebecca to the floor.

"Did it go out the back door?" Clio shouted.

"Not past me!" Maggie called. "Didn't it go out the front?"

"No! Where is it?"

Rebecca ran toward the front door. "You mean it's gone already?"

"I'll check the windows," Tanya said. The girls split up and began a search of the first floor.

Rebecca stopped. "I think I know where it went." She ran for the stairs. The other girls started to follow. "Wait here," she said, "and be ready to run." Rebecca noticed a streak of slime at the top of the banister as she sprinted past to Kyle's room.

She felt the squish of crushed vegetation beneath her feet as she walked through the threshold, brushing away the clammy tendrils of cobweb that clung to her face. The changeling stood in Kyle's crib, its mushroomed hands gripping the rail and its malformed face twisted into a silent howl of rage and anguish. A deluge of bright red maple leaves spilled out of the crib like blood from a wound.

In that moment, Rebecca felt not just horror but pity as well. The changeling was obviously suffering in some way. Maybe by helping Kyle, she could help this poor creature, too. "Hey, little one, I know you're scared and you want to go home. Let us help you. We can take you home."

The changeling turned and fixated on her face. Rebecca gave a cautious smile and reached out to the creature. "Why don't you take my hand and we'll go together?" She walked slowly toward the creature, wading through the rising pile of leaves that still poured from the crib.

As she got closer, the flood of leaves stopped. The house was completely silent. No creaking wood, no ticking clocks. No hiss of anxious girls whispering below. Just the gentle rustle of her legs brushing through the knee-high crimson carpet. One step closer. There. She could almost touch the misshapen white hand that gripped the rail of the crib.

The changeling crouched uncertainly. It lifted one hand from the railing and slowly stretched it toward Rebecca. She could feel the cool velvet of the mushroom caps as the creature's fingertips brushed against hers. "Come on, little one," she whispered. "Let's get you home."

The changeling's fingers clamped over her wrist with a viselike grip, and it let out a piercing wail that brought Rebecca to her knees. Leaves came rushing out of the crib, covering her. She choked on their damp smell and struggled to free herself from the creature's grip, but it was too strong. As the rising tide of foliage covered her face, Rebecca began to panic. Leaves blocked her eyes and mouth. They pressed against her nostrils and slapped against her ears. Rebecca used her free arm to claw them from her face—to sweep them away so that she could see or hear. But with every brush of her arm, still more spilled from between the slats of the crib.

With a final crushing squeeze, the change-ling's grip released, and Rebecca jerked her arm free. She struggled against the growing weight on top of her, desperate for air, drowning in red. She was unprepared for the rake of talons against her shoulders, and she screamed as they tore at her, pushing down sharply, forcing her head to the floor. The changeling's claws dug in and pushed off hard, and she heard the crash of a lamp across the room.

The shower of leaves stopped.

Rebecca quickly dug herself out of the pile and stood up, dazed and gasping for air. Damp leaves filled the room to above her waist. Kyle's favorite lamp, the one that was shaped like a sheep, lay on its side on the table next to the open window. The screen was torn open, and familiar handprints streaked the sill.

The changeling was gone.

CHAPTER 15

REBECCA FLEW DOWNSTAIRS. "It went out Kyle's window! Come on!"

Maggie grabbed Rebecca's arm. "Wait, Rebecca! You're bleeding! What happened?"

"I'm fine; we'll take care of it later. Hurry!"

The four girls ran out the front door and over to the yard beneath Kyle's window. A slippery new patch of slime mold grew in the spot where the changeling had landed. Several white termite grubs wriggled nearby.

Tanya crouched down to unzip her backpack and pulled out a small, cylindrical lamp.

"What is that?" Maggie asked.

"It's my tracker," Tanya said. "I just need to set it up."

"So which way did it go?" Clio asked, looking around.

"It must be long gone by now," Maggie said.

"I don't think so." Rebecca scanned the surrounding forest. She could still feel the changeling nearby, watching them. She heard the rustle of branches and turned to see a flash of movement in the bushes at the forest's edge. "Over there!"

"Don't wait for me," Tanya said. "You're the chasers, remember? I'm just the backup plan. Don't worry. I'll find you. Go!"

The other girls ran toward the changeling, who scampered away and grabbed a low-hanging branch to swing onto a nearby tree.

"Nobody said it could swing around like a monkey!" Maggie said, already panting. "How are we going to catch it now? I mean, have you ever heard of anyone actually catching a monkey?"

"Leopards do," Clio answered, "but we don't need to catch it; we just have to follow it. Keep moving!" She picked up her pace and darted forward, Rebecca at her side. Maggie followed.

Clio and Rebecca raced behind the changeling, managing to keep up just enough to hold it in their line of sight. Its wiry limbs and taloned feet scuttled through the foliage, allowing the creature to leap easily from tree to tree.

Maggie puffed along behind them, pausing occasionally to massage the stitch in her side. Finally she stopped. "I'm beat. You guys keep moving. I'll wait for Tanya."

Rebecca and Clio nodded and pushed forward, sprinting now to keep pace with the creature. The pale silhouette of Maggie faded in the distance behind them, and the forest grew thicker. Soon the treetops knit together so tightly that the moonlight no longer filtered through to the forest floor. The girls' eyes struggled to follow the faint shape above them.

There was a crash from a nearby tree, and the

changeling dropped like a stone. It landed with a sickening thud like an ax on rotten wood, and the girls stopped, stunned. They crept forward cautiously. "Is it dead?" Clio asked.

"It can't be," Rebecca said anxiously. "We need it alive; otherwise we'll never find Kyle!"

With a harsh grunt, the creature lurched up and the girls jumped back, startled. A small scream escaped from Rebecca's lips, but the changeling didn't even seem to hear her. It shook itself, then padded off unsteadily toward the heart of the forest, moving with a lopsided gait.

"I think it might be hurt," Rebecca said. "It's slowed down some. Poor thing."

"Poor thing?! That little monster?" Clio shuddered. "I'm just happy we don't have to sprint anymore. I don't think I could have kept up that pace much longer."

As the girls jogged quietly behind the limping creature, Rebecca listened for Maggie and Tanya. She thought she heard brush crashing somewhere nearby, but she couldn't be sure.

Just ahead of them, the changeling stopped

near a patch of brightly colored mushrooms. It plucked several and scarfed them down greedily.

"What's it doing? Aren't those poisonous?" Rebecca whispered.

"I don't think anything's poisonous for *that*. I mean, it's half fungus or something already anyway."

After stuffing several more mushrooms into its mouth, the changeling stretched up to its full two-foot height and began hopping up and down. Rebecca groaned inwardly and braced herself to run. Seconds later, the changeling took off like a shot.

"What just happened?!" Clio asked.

"I think it just powered up!" Rebecca said.

She took off in a dead sprint with Clio at her heels, but after a few minutes they could no longer see the creature in front of them. Rebecca finally slowed to a stop and bent forward at the waist, struggling to catch her breath. "Dang it; it's no use now. It's gone."

Clio collapsed on the damp ground next to her,

panting. "Don't worry; we still have our backup plan."

"Assuming they can actually find us."

"This is Tanya we're talking about, remember? They'll find us."

Rebecca pulled a flashlight out of her pocket and waved it around over her head. "Hopefully this will help," she said. The crashing grew louder, and she caught a glimpse of a purplish light twinkling between the trees. "Over here, you guys! Hurry!"

Every second waiting felt like an eternity to Rebecca. She tried not to think about what would happen if the changeling got so far ahead of them that they couldn't find it. Without the changeling, they would never be able to find Kyle. *That won't happen*, she told herself. *I won't let that happen*.

The light grew brighter, and soon Rebecca could hear Tanya's and Maggie's voices as they grew closer, treading carefully through the underbrush. Rebecca clapped her hands impatiently. "Come on! Let's go! It's getting away!"

"We're coming!" Maggie called. "And by the way, you're welcome for us finding you and everything. We only just tracked you for, like, ever through these dark woods that are probably filled with snakes and bears or whatever. Oh, right, and monsters and stuff. You know, no big deal!"

Rebecca bounced on the balls of her feet. "I promise you when this is all over I will write you all very long thank-you notes and give you medals, but for right now, can we please get moving? Who knows where that thing could be by now?"

"I vote for brownies instead of medals. No wait—carrot cake," Tanya said, testing the switch on a purplish light she held in her hand.

"Carrot cake? Why would you . . . ? You know what, I can't even. Seriously, only you would say that," Maggie said.

Clio laughed. "I love carrot cake, too!"

"Don't encourage her," Maggie said.

Rebecca threw up her hands.

Maggie grinned. "Now if everyone's ready, let's get going before Becks here explodes or something."

"Thank you! You good to go, Tanya?"

Tanya held up the purplish light. "Let's do this! Now, where did you last see that little beastie?" Rebecca pointed. Tanya shone the light over the spot, illuminating a glowing splotch with a set of birdlike footprints leading away from it.

"No way!" Clio said, and the girls rushed forward to follow the footprints. "It's like following a trail of bread crumbs! How did you build it?"

Tanya held the light out in front of them as the girls jogged along. "This is just a black light. I remembered that last summer, when my dad was growing tomatoes, we used one to find tomato hornworms. You can't really see them normally, but they totally glow under UV light! There's a whole list of things that do that, including rotten stuff and mold. Presto!"

"Rotten stuff and mold . . . yup, sounds like a changeling, all right!" Maggie said.

"Don't forget teeth!" Clio added.

"There's always *something* rotten in a changeling, especially if it's been charmed for a while," Tanya explained. "They're not really made to stay in human form that long, so they start to decay."

"That's sad," Rebecca said. "Their human life is over before it's even really begun."

Maggie rolled her eyes. "Don't go feeling sorry for it, Becks. We've been running through the woods for miles after this stupid thing. This is worse than gym class!"

The girls laughed, but Tanya shushed them. They stood in the middle of a large clearing lit by silvery moonlight. "Hang on. It's stopped."

"What do you mean?" Clio asked.

"Look! The trail ends here."

Rebecca searched the ground. "But it can't just end! Everyone spread out and start looking. We have to be close."

Clio checked her watch. "Only three hours until the Dunmores get home."

"This just keeps getting better and better!" Maggie said. Then she noticed Rebecca's drawn face, and her voice lowered. "Don't worry, Becks. We'll get him back."

Rebecca walked toward a small brook burbling

at the edge of the clearing. She could see the distorted reflection of the full moon on the water's surface. Following the brook upstream, she searched for footprints or tracks, but she found none. As she crept along, Rebecca noticed that the brook grew narrower, until the water seemed to disappear into the ground.

Surprised, Rebecca looked closer. The brook seemed to spring from the base of a massive yew tree. The tree was ancient and twisted, with roots extending like rough tentacles. Its long branches stretched far overhead, thick with leaves that shrouded the forest floor in darkness. Rebecca ran her hands over the rough bark and along the opening where the stream bubbled out. It felt almost as large as a small cave. Or a doorway.

"You guys! Over here!" Rebecca called. The girls hurried to the tree, and Rebecca pointed to the hollow. "Tanya, can you shine the black light into the opening?"

Tanya held up the light, and the changeling's distinctive tracks smeared the edges of the hollow. Tanya reached forward. Her hand touched only air. "There's no back wall," she said. "It's not a hollow; it's a portal."

"It's *the* portal." Clio grinned. "We found the entrance to the Nightmare Realm." Her smile faded. "Once we go through, there's no turning back. If anyone wants to change their mind, now is the time to do it. No harm, no foul."

Rebecca looked carefully at the other girls' faces, waiting. She saw fear there, but no one spoke. "Thank you," she whispered, looking at each of her friends. "I won't let you down. I promise."

The girls stripped off their shoes and socks and stepped into the water. Rebecca gasped; it was as cold as fresh snowmelt. Tanya extinguished her light and tucked it back in her pack.

Picking carefully between the slippery stones, the girls stepped one by one into the velvety black opening and disappeared from view.

CHAPTER
16

IT WAS INKY black inside the tunnel. Treading slowly along the stream's rocky bottom, Rebecca trailed her right hand across the wall of the passage and waved the left in front of her to feel for obstacles. Clio's fingers rested lightly on her left shoulder. The only sound was the splash of their footsteps over the gentle babbling of the water.

Silent with concentration, the girls pushed against the current and moved slowly downward. Tanya let out a small exclamation of surprise.

"What is it?" Rebecca asked.

"The water. It's flowing *uphill*. That's just . . . wrong."

"Welcome to the Nightmare Realm," Maggie said softly.

The rough wood of the wall gradually changed to something slippery and wet that seemed to squirm beneath Rebecca's fingertips. She snatched her hand away. Soon, a sickly yellow light suffused the passage in front of them, and the rocky stream bottom gave way to warm, wet slime that sucked at their feet. As they drew closer to the light, she noticed twisted figures carved into the slick walls: skeletal men with panther heads, an eyeless child with black wings. She pointed and heard Clio grunt behind her.

"*Lusus naturae*," Clio whispered. Maggie moaned faintly behind her.

At the edge of her hearing, Rebecca could just make out a faint, pulsating sound that throbbed like a heartbeat. It curled through the passage and pulled her forward. Drums.

As they reached the end of the tunnel, the drumming grew louder, until Rebecca and Clio stepped into the shadows at the edge of a moonlit clearing. Rebecca looked behind her and saw the same yew tree behind them, but now the trunk was scarred and black, its leafless limbs twisting like the arms of some giant, ancient monster. The clearing looked exactly like the spot they had left, only everything was dark and diseased, the rocks covered in slimy black moss, the brook choked with foamy scum.

She scanned the clearing, searching for Kyle.

In the center of the clearing, misshapen creatures grouped around the crackling flames of a bonfire. Some of them danced, their skeletal limbs twisting above their heads, weaving around one another like snakes. Peeling skin fluttered in the shifting light. One's eyeless face was streaked with black mildew. Another turned, and as the firelight caught its features, Rebecca saw only a seamless patch of skin where the mouth should be.

Then she saw him, a bright little bundle cuddled in a cradle of twisted branches. Kyle. Was he all right? Several lusus cooed over him, rocking the cradle gently. Long, slender fingers, white as bleached bone, reached in and stroked his cheek. Rebecca hurried forward, but Clio grabbed her arm.

"Hold up. Take a breath. He's safe. We need to stick to our plan."

Tanya and Maggie crept out of the tunnel to join them, and the girls huddled together. "Remember what we know about the Night Queen," Tanya said. "The lusus hate to lose, and they never play fair. The only way we'll get Kyle back is if we outsmart her."

"Don't worry," Maggie said, her voice shaking. She touched Rebecca's shoulder. "They can't be that smart. Who would want to just sit on a bunch of rocks listening to some lame drum circle?" She let out a hollow laugh, her eyes wide with fear. "I mean, duh! Haven't they ever heard of the internet? They could have a way better setup out here."

Rebecca squeezed Maggie's hand, and the girls stepped into the moonlight. Immediately the drumming stopped. The lusus dropped their arms and stared at the intruders with a cold, hostile curiosity.

The crowd parted as the girls approached the bonfire, making the narrowest of paths for them to walk through. Rebecca had to force herself not to shrink back when she accidentally brushed against a scaly arm.

The cluster opened up to reveal a dais framed with maple trees, their tired, bent trunks crusted with scallops of yellow fungus. Heavy with foliage, their intertwined, drooping branches created a crimson arbor draped with cobwebs. The stone floor of the dais below was carpeted with fallen red leaves.

There, in the center of the dais, the Night Queen sat on a throne of broken marble tombstones, the carvings barely visible beneath the moss that streaked its pitted surface. The queen's skin was a deep twilight blue, sprinkled with tiny twinkling stars. Brittle, jointed tendrils spilled from her head. They chittered as she moved, scrabbling at her shoulders, and Rebecca felt Maggie sag against her. "Oh, God, her hair. What is it?"

Tanya squeezed in closer. "It's . . . it looks like spiders' legs."

"Just try not to think about it," Clio whispered.

The jointed legs of the queen's hair reached up to adjust a crown of curving, silver ram's horns tipped with jet-black stones. Beneath her mantle of dusty owl feathers, her long gown glowed sallowly in the firelight, the sour yellow-white of stained teeth. Animal bones studded the bodice and skirt, and the heavy hem was trimmed with matted fur that had faded to a dull, greasy gray. The changeling huddled brokenly at her feet.

The four girls joined hands and stepped forward. Remembering the formal speech from the books, Rebecca allowed her voice to ring throughout the clearing. "We have come to claim the babe." An agitated whispering rose up around them.

"Silence!" the Night Queen commanded, her teeth gleaming in the moonlight like black pearls. The whispering stopped. The queen stared down at the girls; her golden eyes filled with disdain. "What makes you believe you have the right to be here?"

The other lusus tittered. Rebecca saw a hot

flush forming on Maggie's cheeks. Her friend stood taller, eyes narrowing.

"Mean girl," Maggie said under her breath.

"Huh?" Rebecca whispered back. Maggie simply grunted in response.

The queen raised her arms, palms upward, and faced the crowd. "Have they come with gifts for us? Have they carried payment?" The crowd behind the girls pushed forward to see what the girls had brought.

Clio took another step forward. "No payment," she said firmly. "No gifts. The babe is ours by right."

The Night Queen stood, her face twisted in a mocking smile. The changeling clung to her skirts, and she casually kicked it away. "These worthless girls come to claim our property. They bring us no payment. They offer no gifts. And yet they speak to us of rights."

The creatures hissed and moved closer to the girls, encircling them. The queen reached into Kyle's cradle and lifted him into her arms. "Only a fool would advise a mortal to come to us offering nothing but arrogant demands." She studied Clio's face for a long moment. "We are bored with you. Begone," she called dismissively. The creatures laughed and began prodding the girls away from the fire, back toward the yew tree. The queen turned back to her throne.

"Hey!" Maggie said, slapping at the furry hand that pinched her arm. "We're not finished yet!" She shoved her way toward the dais, the other girls following close behind her. One of the lusus cackled and yanked Rebecca's hair. She gritted her teeth and pulled it out of the creature's grasp.

"Wait! We do have something to offer!" Rebecca called to the retreating queen's back. The queen stopped.

"We are listening," she said.

"A game," Tanya said.

The queen turned around. "A game?" she asked. Her hair moved restlessly. "We like games."

"It's simple," Clio said. "You give us three challenges. If we defeat you in all three challenges, we take Kyle and go. And if we don't . . ." Her voice faltered.

"If we don't," Rebecca continued, "the babe stays."

The queen handed Kyle to her attendants and sat back on her throne. "We like this game," she said, "but the babe is not enough." Her eyes glittered with greed and another expression that Rebecca couldn't identify. "If our challenges are not met, we also keep the girls." She looked down at her sleeve and brushed a spider off its cuff. "We are in need of more servants; they keep dying." She gestured, and an attendant brought forward a large silver mirror and held it up. The queen studied her reflection and plucked at the bones on her bodice. "Do our guests accept?"

The girls formed a tight huddle. "Whoa, I don't like this at all. This is not what we talked about," Maggie said. "Did you see that look on her face? There's no way she's going to let us walk out of here."

"We have no choice," Rebecca said. "I'm not leaving without Kyle."

"Yeah, but being her prisoners? Death?" Maggie asked. "That wasn't part of the plan."

"Yeah, well, no plan is perfect," Tanya said.

"Yours are! They're always perfect! So why all of a sudden does this one particular plan have to be the one with the flaw? Seriously, couldn't we save that for something that *doesn't* end our lives forever?"

"Hey, most of our plans don't involve supernatural beings, so cut us a little slack," Tanya said. "We knew something like this could happen."

"Look, let's take a vote," Clio suggested. "All in favor of accepting her terms?" Rebecca raised her hand. Tanya and Clio followed.

Maggie folded her arms, then slowly raised her hand. "If I come back without you guys, I'll be dead anyway. But I'm telling you, we can't trust her."

Rebecca nodded to the other girls and turned to face the queen. "We accept."

CHAPTER 17

"IT'S GOING TO be a riddle. The first one is always a riddle," Clio whispered.

The queen rose and addressed the crowd. "The first challenge shall be a riddle."

Clio pumped her fist. "Yessss! I knew it!" She bounced up and down on the balls of her feet and loosened her shoulders like a boxer, flexing her fingers.

"Wow, someone's pretty confident," Maggie said.

"Shhh!" Tanya said. The queen moved forward on the dais and stood over the girls, looking down on them like a hawk over its prey. The stars on her skin glittered.

> *"Window of night*
> *Wolves' delight*
> *Harvest's bride*
> *I beckon the tide*
> *Who am I?"*

The girls put their heads together. "Could it be a sheep?" Maggie asked.

"A sheep? Why would it be a sheep?" Tanya said.

"She said 'wolves' delight.' Wolves love sheep!"

"Yeah, but what about the rest of the riddle?"

"Well, maybe the night part is like you count sheep at night to help you sleep. And the harvest could be, like, a feast or something. People ate sheep in olden times a lot, didn't they?"

"People still eat sheep, Mags. It's called lamb," Tanya said.

"See, so that makes even more sense. It's got to be sheep!"

Rebecca folded her arms. "But wait, sheep have nothing to do with the tides. I don't think that's right."

"But maybe the sheep is, like, playing on the beach or something. You know, chasing the water like a dog does."

"That's getting a little weird," Rebecca said.

"Whatever. It's definitely a sheep," Maggie said.

"Enough with the sheep! It's not a sheep!" Tanya said.

"Fine. Then what else could it be?" Maggie asked.

Clio clapped her hands triumphantly. "Wait! I've got it! It's the moon!"

A slow smile spread across Tanya's face. "Of course! The tides! Why didn't I think of that?" She paused, thinking. "But wait, last week I read this article about wolves, and scientists have discovered that they don't actually howl at the moon."

Maggie gestured to the clearing around them. "Um, in case you haven't noticed, we're trying to solve a riddle given to us by a magical blue lady with actual stars on her skin. Not tattoos of stars.

Actual stars. Do you really think science has anything to do with this?"

Rebecca ran the riddle through her head again. The moon could definitely be the queen of the night, and—forgetting Tanya's article—wolves certainly had some kind of connection to the moon. There was always the harvest moon in the fall, and of course she knew that the moon controlled the tides. "I think Clio's right," she said.

"I guess, but I still think a sheep would be much more awesome. But, yeah, Clio's the riddle master. So let's go with the moon," Maggie said.

Tanya grinned. "I guess it's possible that the Night Queen didn't read that article last month. Well played, Clio."

Clio stepped forward confidently. "Our answer is the moon." The lusus pressed in eagerly, malice in their eyes.

A look of irritation crossed the Night Queen's perfect features. "It is the moon." The creatures hissed in disappointment, and Clio yelped as a wet, boneless tentacle snaked out of the crowd and twisted her ear.

The queen arranged her face into a regal smile and raised her arms above her head. "In honor of the first victory, we shall reward our challengers with a banquet." The drummers began to play, and the lusus danced in a lurching circle around the girls.

A long table covered with black silk rose out of the ground, its surface laden with silver platters piled high with delicious treats. Rebecca spied delicate white mini-cupcakes with fluffy pink icing, gooey cheese pizza with a perfect, golden-brown crust, and an elaborate gingerbread house covered in candy. Enormous ice cream sundaes in frosted glass bowls sat between silver baskets of crispy fried chicken and pyramids of fresh, juicy cheeseburgers. There was even a chocolate fountain in the middle.

Rebecca could smell every sumptuous dish, each aroma more delicious than the next. She tried to remember when she had last eaten; it must have been hours ago. She didn't think she had ever been so hungry. Rebecca's mind felt fuzzy and slow, and all she could think about was the blissful sweetness of icing melting on her tongue. She should definitely eat something so that her mind could focus on defeating the queen. It would be easier to win the challenges if she wasn't so hungry; she was sure of it.

The table settled itself and the girls rushed over to it. Tanya picked up a wooden plate and reached for a slice of pizza. Rebecca went straight for the cupcakes. Maggie grabbed her arm. "Wait a minute. Something's not right."

"What do you mean?"

Maggie nodded at the queen, who stood watching them with interest. "Look at her. You saw her face when we answered that riddle. She was not a happy camper."

Tanya's hand hovered above the steaming slice of pizza. "Yeah, so? She's just being a good sport."

Maggie lowered her voice. "Good sport? Really? Snap out of it! This is the Night Queen we're talking about, remember? Do you really want to eat that food?"

Tanya's hand moved closer to the pizza. "Well, yeah, we kind of do."

Rebecca pulled her arm out of Maggie's grip.

"Look, there's nothing wrong with it. Here, smell this cupcake."

Maggie waved the cupcake away. "I'm not going to smell your cupcake, weirdo. Focus."

"I don't want to focus. I'm starving!"

Maggie raised her voice. "Clio, you're with me, right? Can you help me talk some sense into these two?" Clio didn't answer. She had plunged her arms up to the elbows into a huge china bowl filled with jelly beans. The drumbeats grew faster and louder; the creatures' dancing, more frenzied. Jelly beans spilled from Clio's cupped hands as she brought them to her mouth.

"No!" Maggie ran over and slapped Clio's hands away. The candies scattered across the table. Rebecca forgot her cupcake for a moment.

Clio shoved Maggie. "Hey! What was that about?! Those were *my* jelly beans!"

Tanya curled her lip and hunched over the pizza, guarding it. "Stop trying to take our food. Get your own!" On the dais behind them, the Night Queen let out a tinkling laugh and clapped her hands.

Rebecca looked again at the cupcakes. The dollops of pink frosting, spotted with rainbow sprinkles. The scalloped edges of the cakes so perfect. Her mouth watered. *I've worked really hard. I deserve those cupcakes. Why is Maggie trying to ruin everything?*

Maggie pushed her way between the other girls and stood with her back to the table, arms spread open to block her friends from the food. "Just stop and think about it, please! Do any stories end with the Night Queen just randomly doing something nice? She's mean to the bone, and I may not know much about ghost stories, but I do know mean girls. Don't you guys ever watch TV? I'm telling you, this is a trick!"

"I don't care. I'm hungry!" Clio edged closer to the table.

In desperation Maggie bent over and grabbed a handful of dirt from the clearing floor. She threw it over the jelly beans, covering them with clods of soil.

"What are you doing?!"

Maggie grabbed two more handfuls, tossing

them on the pizza and cupcakes. "No way am I going to let you eat this." She tipped over the plate of burgers, spilling them off the table. As soon as the burgers touched the ground, they broke apart, transforming into piles of wriggling worms and heavy black beetles. The three girls jumped back, their faces pale. The fog in Rebecca's head cleared.

"Still hungry?" Maggie asked. Rebecca thought about how close she had come to eating those cup-cakes, and she gagged. Tanya shuddered, and Clio wiped her hands on her jeans. Maggie turned to the dais. "Yeah, thanks, but I think we're going to pass on the banquet. We're not really hungry."

The music stopped abruptly. The table sank slowly back down into the earth, the food trans-forming into insects that skittered across the girls' toes before scuttling away under the leaves. The queen sat rigid upon her throne, her face a mask of cold stone. Rebecca saw her fingers tighten slightly on the throne's arms, then loosen again. Her chitinous locks scratched angrily against her shoulders. The grimacing changeling cowered at her feet, and the other lusus backed away, whispering, widening the circle around the girls.

The queen stood. "You met the second challenge by refusing to eat."

The girls hugged one another, their faces glowing with relief. "Yes!" Clio whispered. "Two down. Just one more to go."

The queen's face shifted into a brief, tight smile. "There is but one challenge remaining. If it is met, the girls are free to take the babe and go. If it is not, all will remain with us." The lusus tittered. Rebecca could sense their excitement. They knew the end was close.

The Night Queen gestured to her attendants, and one of them lifted Kyle from the cradle and placed him in the queen's arms. Rebecca's heart tightened in her chest. "For the final challenge, our guests must set right the balance of nature. In order to win the babe, they must sacrifice the changeling. For the children to leave freely, the changeling must be thrown into the fire."

CHAPTER 18

THE CHANGELING SHRIEKED and clung to the Night Queen's skirts, as if begging for mercy. She kicked it away savagely, and Kyle began to cry. The queen's lip curled in disgust. She shoved Kyle into the arms of a waiting attendant, who then disappeared into the shadows.

The changeling lurched toward the edge of the dais and leaped awkwardly to the ground below. It limped toward the forest's edge, desperate to escape, but the night creatures surrounded it. Several began to tease it, poking at it with sticks and laughing as it feebly snapped its teeth at them.

A gray skeleton with the head of a shaggy black wolf carried a gilded cage over to the group, and the lusus forced the changeling inside. Trapped, its ugly face twisted into a howl of fear and rage. Two cadavers hooked a long silver pole onto the top of the cage and hung it near the dais. The creature's decaying hands shook the golden bars in vain.

The girls stood frozen. Rebecca could hear Kyle's cries growing fainter as the attendant soothed him. The changeling's cries weakened as well, softening to a dull whimper.

The Night Queen ignored the chaos around her. She sat in front of the mirror again, watching her reflection as several attendants placed a heavy, jet necklace at her throat.

Tanya was the first to speak. Her voice was unsteady. "It probably shouldn't be too hard, right?" She swallowed. "After all, it's really just an old log, isn't it? It's not like it's an actual animal. Or a person."

"Yeah," Clio said. "And it's nasty, anyway. It hurt us anytime it had the chance, remember? It's a monster. You're supposed to kill monsters."

Rebecca remembered the wiry grip of the changeling's hands on her wrists and the terror she had felt back in Kyle's bedroom. Her back burned from where talons had cut her.

"It's not like we'd even be killing it, anyway," Maggie said. She picked up a twig from the ground and turned it over in her hands. "I mean, is it even really alive? Aren't we just . . . you know . . . making it turn back into a log or whatever it was before?"

"Besides," Tanya added, "look at it. I think it's already dying." The girls watched the changeling, who huddled, shivering at the bottom of its cage. One of its arms jutted out from its body at an odd angle. "Maybe we would actually be helping it, like putting it out of its misery."

"If it's the only way to bring Kyle home, we have to do it," Rebecca said. "We don't have a choice." She walked over to the bonfire and held out her hands, stretching her fingers over the hot flames. The fire crackled; the wood beneath glowed red. Embers drifted upward into the night sky. *All we would be doing is just tossing a piece of wood into a fire. I've done that a million times. It's not like it's one of us. It's only a log.* The whole thing would take less than a minute, and then Kyle would be back safely in her arms. They could all go home.

She could see the Night Queen's reflection in the mirror. The queen spoke softly to her attendants and adjusted the necklace at her throat, but the golden eyes followed Rebecca.

Rebecca walked over to the cage and bent down, looking inside. The changeling hissed and snapped at her, scraping its talons along the bottom of the cage. There was furry mold on its face, and a thick, yellow liquid dripped from its injured arm. It swiped at her with its good arm, and Rebecca flinched. The creature managed a wheezing giggle.

The girls crowded in behind her. "So should we just grab it and, you know, toss it in?" Maggie asked.

"I don't want to get bitten or scratched again. It could still really hurt us," Clio said. "Maybe we could carry the whole cage over and then just kind of dump it in."

Tanya folded her arms. "Maybe . . . but that seems sort of, I don't know . . . mean."

"What's there to be mean about?" Maggie said. "Think of it like we're killing a bug. You see a bug in your room, you hurry up and squish it. You don't think about how to do it *nicely*."

"Yeah, but I don't kill bugs. I catch them with a cup and put them outside again," Tanya said.

Clio looked at her watch. "Well, however we do it, it has to be quick. We have less than an hour until Kyle's parents get home."

Rebecca stretched her neck to try to find the attendant holding Kyle, but the baby was back in the cradle, dozing. He looked so small and vulnerable. "Look, you guys," she said to her friends. "I brought us here; it's my responsibility. I'll do it."

The other girls backed up as Rebecca bent down and opened the cage door. The changeling cowered against the opposite wall, hissing. She reached inside, carefully avoiding the creature's injuries, and scooped it into her arms. The changeling bit and scratched at her, but it seemed to know that all was lost. The teeth barely grazed her skin. After a few moments of weak struggles, it lay limply in her arms, the bulbous head resting on her shoulder. She could hear its breathing, thick and wet, near her ear.

Without thinking, Rebecca murmured to the changeling the way she would to any frightened baby. "Shh . . . shh . . . I know you're scared, I know. It's all right." She stroked its rotting back. "In just a few minutes, it will all be over."

As she turned toward the fire, everything slowed. The shifting light of the flames bathed her friends' stricken faces in flickering shadows of red and gold. The night creatures stilled; their conversations fell away, and their hollow eyes glinted with malicious curiosity. The distance to the fire seemed to stretch impossibly. Her legs quivered, and a wave of exhaustion washed over her. Rebecca took the first trembling step toward the fire, and the queen stood up from her throne. Her forgotten attendants stepped back.

Rebecca forced her leaden legs to take another step, the changeling in her arms weighing her down like a stone. Her body seemed to be rebelling against her, pulling her backward, away from the fire. Nothing in this dark world felt right, but this was a deeper kind of wrong. Something nagged at the edge of her mind, struggling to the surface.

Rebecca took another step, and from the corner of her eye she caught a glint of gleaming black teeth. For just one second, a tight smile of triumph flashed across the queen's face. But the smile disappeared as quickly as it had come, and Rebecca wondered if she had even seen it at all. She tightened her jaw. Only the Night Queen would be cruel enough to take pleasure in something like this.

If I have to do this, I'm not going to let her make it ugly. Rebecca unconsciously began to hum a lullaby to the pitiful creature in her arms. Her heart drummed in time, and she allowed herself to draw strength from the melody. The heavy feeling left her body, but the deep sense of unease remained.

Rebecca took another step. Why would the queen free them this way? Why did she want them to kill the changeling?

Because she thinks I can't; that's why. She thinks I'm not strong enough to do it.

Rebecca stepped closer to the bonfire.

The logs in the fire shifted, and an ember leaped out of the flames with a loud pop. She jumped, and the changeling trembled in her arms.

Will it feel anything? What if it screams? I don't think I can do it if it's going to scream.

Rebecca stopped. She took a deep breath and steeled herself.

I cannot let her win.

She moved a step closer.

I have to be as cruel as she is. That's the only way to beat her.

The memory surfaced, flashing like a beacon. Clio, standing in the shop, reading from a scroll. The poem.

> *"Cruelty is as cruelty does*
> *But none can rule the heart that loves."*

Rebecca walked the final few feet to the fire and looked back at the dais.

Why did the queen smile when she saw me walk toward the fire? Why would she smile if she's about to lose?

She felt the heat from the blaze and looked down into the heart of the flames. Rebecca tried to imagine what it would feel like to put the changeling on the burning pyre. Could she really do it? In one agonizing moment, it would all be over. For all of them.

She imagined Kyle in her arms and her friends surrounding them. Their relieved faces lit by the glow of the fire, the flames strong and tall from the extra fuel. The fuel she carried in her arms.

Cruelty is as cruelty does.

Rebecca did not know if she could bear to be this cruel, even to save her friends. Even to save Kyle.

But I have to save them. I have to. There's no one else but me.

Her heart cried out against what she was about to do.

None can rule the heart that loves.

Tears spilled down her cheeks.

She would do it quickly, before she had time to think.

Why did the queen smile?

Rebecca closed her eyes.

Why did she smile?

Now.

She would do it now.

CHAPTER 19

REBECCA'S ARMS TIGHTENED around the creature, hugging it to her chest. Without looking at anyone else, she turned and sprinted away from the fire, toward the edge of the clearing. The changeling clung to her. She had no idea if her gamble would work, but she had to risk it. She just needed to make it to the yew tree before the lusus caught up with her.

Rebecca reached the tree and placed the changeling in the stream near its entrance. "Hurry! Go through the tree and hide in the forest! They won't have time to find you before the portal closes again!" The changeling scampered through the opening without even pausing to look back at her in thanks.

Rebecca turned to face the clearing and stood firmly in front of the portal, guarding it from the creatures that now formed a tight circle around her. Several darted toward her, and she spread her arms wide, blocking their way into the opening. She knew she had no chance of stopping them, but at least she might buy enough time for the changeling to get through the tunnel and find a place to hide. Rebecca squeezed her eyes shut and braced herself, preparing for an onslaught of attacks.

A few seconds passed. Nothing happened.

She opened her eyes to find that the lusus still surrounded her, but none of them moved in for a fight. Rebecca eyed the creatures warily, her hands balled into fists. Had it worked? Had she been right? Maybe they had decided the changeling just wasn't worth the risk of being trapped in the other world. They must have known that it didn't have long to live; it probably didn't make any difference to them where it died.

Rebecca looked back to see her friends standing on the dais, surrounded by the queen and her attendants. They were chaining the girls' wrists. Even from a distance, Rebecca could see the look of shock and betrayal on her friends' faces. She felt all the fight go out of her. She had been wrong. Her heart sank when she realized the enormity of what she had done—she had just risked her life and the lives of her friends to save a monster that was going to die anyway, and all because of some stupid hunch. Why hadn't she just stuck with the plan?

And what about Kyle? He was reasonably safe now, but how long would that last? She knew the Night Queen would tire of him eventually, and what would happen to him then? Rebecca followed the lusus back to the bonfire. *How could I think I could outsmart her? The only way to beat her at her own game is to be tougher than she is. And I wasn't. I failed.*

The Night Queen was beautiful and terrifying in her triumph. She held a twisted bone scepter in her right hand, and her voice was resonant with the thrill of her victory. "Our guests have failed the last challenge. All now belong to us."

Behind her, Maggie, Clio, and Tanya stood with shoulders hunched in defeat. The tarnished silver chains hung limply from their wrists, and their faces were ashen and bleak with despair. Without any prodding, Rebecca stepped up on the dais to join them. It was her fault her friends were standing here.

A part of her still hoped she could find some way to undo what had happened, or at least persuade the Night Queen to let the others go. Maybe she could still protect them. *Yeah, like the way I protected Kyle? I had the chance to save him, and I blew it. There's nothing I can do for anyone now.* With tears spilling down her cheeks, Rebecca could barely raise her head to face her friends. "I'm sorry; I'm so sorry. I just couldn't believe it was the way to win," she whispered. "I thought there had to be another way."

Tanya was crying, too. "I don't think I could have done it, either," she whispered back.

"I could have," Maggie said. "I hated that thing!" Her voice was choked with hurt. "Rebecca, why didn't you just ask me to do it?"

"I don't know," Rebecca said miserably. "I just felt like it had to be me. It felt like I was doing the right thing."

"I guess doing the right thing isn't always the way to win," Clio said. Her voice broke. "It's just that we worked so hard, Rebecca! We had a plan. I thought we had this! I thought we were a team."

"I know," Rebecca said. "We are. But . . . I can't explain it. It was something about that poem, the one from the scroll. I just kept hearing it in my head: *Cruelty is as cruelty does, but none—*"

The scepter rung out hollowly as the queen rapped it on the dais floor. "Silence!" She turned to her guards. "Wolf Head! Chain the girl!"

Rebecca held out her arms, and the wolf-headed lusus brought forward a set of silver cuffs connected by a heavy chain. Careful not to touch her, he snapped them around her wrists. Rebecca winced at the feel of the cold metal against her skin. But as she slid her fingers over them, the cuffs split in two and fell from her arms, clattering on the wood below. The lusus erupted into alarmed whispers, and Wolf Head shot a terrified look at the queen.

Rebecca could see the queen was shaken, but the monarch was not about to lose control over her subjects. She raised her scepter, and a hush fell over the crowd. "Bonefingers, get the vines. Bind her," she commanded. Another gray skeleton grabbed a length of vines and began wrapping Rebecca tightly. Rebecca felt like a mummy, her arms rigid against her sides. Every unscratched itch suddenly demanded attention.

"This is dumb. What are they even doing?" Maggie said.

The skeleton stepped away, and Rebecca shifted in place, trying to find a way to get reasonably comfortable. She bent her elbow and stretched her shoulders, working to loosen the tightness around her chest. The vines withered and went limp, sliding off her like dead snakes. Someone in the crowd let out a small scream, and the lusus on the dais instinctively stepped away from her.

"What sorcery is this?" the queen demanded, her eyes flashing with hate.

Still stunned herself, Rebecca faced her wordlessly. Even the attendants seemed too afraid to breathe.

In the silence Rebecca heard a small chuckle behind her. "Now I get it. Oh, that's good!"

"Clio, shh!" Tanya whispered. "Don't make her angrier!"

"She can be angry all she wants," Clio said, "but it won't matter to Rebecca. She can't capture her. She can't touch her!"

"Wicked, wicked lying girl!" the queen said, and reached forward to slap Rebecca. As soon as her hand grazed Rebecca's cheek, the queen shrieked and drew back as if burned. Clio laughed louder.

"That's what that poem meant," Clio said. "Remember? *But none can rule the heart that loves.*' The lusus can't imprison you. They can't control you. They can't make you do anything you don't want to do now."

"But why?" Rebecca asked.

"Not important," Maggie said. "More important: getting us out of here. Do your new magical powers include freeing your friends?"

"I don't know," Rebecca said, and stepped toward the other girls. The Night Queen started forward to block her way, and Rebecca's arm brushed against the queen's gown. Rebecca heard a sizzle, and the queen recoiled, a scorch mark on her yellowed sleeve. Wolf Head grabbed the silver pole from the changeling's cage and swung it at Rebecca's head. She threw up her arms to defend herself, and her hand slapped against the cold metal. The pole shattered into dust, bathing the dais in a cloud of glittering silver. Wolf Head slowly backed away, shocked.

Rebecca moved toward her friends again, and this time no lusus moved to stop her. She touched the cuffs on Maggie's wrists, and they split open and fell to the ground. She quickly freed the other girls, and the four friends hugged one another. "Come on, let's go!" Maggie said, hopping down from the dais.

"Not without Kyle," Rebecca said.

"Shoot! I forgot!"

"Seriously?" Tanya said.

"Well, there was a lot of excitement!" Maggie said.

Rebecca raised her voice to address the crowd formally. "We demand the return of the babe. We have bested the queen in all three challenges, and the babe is to be returned to us by right!"

The night creatures made no move. Rebecca whispered into Tanya's ear. "What do we do now?"

"Try again, maybe?"

"Okay, this is stupid," Maggie said. She walked over to the cradle, reached in, and scooped Kyle into her arms. "Now can we go? I am so over this place!" The queen's face was tight with fury; she turned her back on the girls, her spine rigid.

Kyle squealed and bounced with excitement as soon as he noticed Rebecca. She hurried over and hugged him tightly. "I missed you!" Her eyes blurred with tears as she heard his familiar snuffle in her ear.

Clio checked her watch. "We gotta go, like, right now." The girls ran across the clearing toward the portal. The lusus silently parted to let them through, their faces like stone.

As the girls reached the yew tree, the queen's icy voice cut through the clearing. "*Lusus naturae* never forgive. And we never forget."

CHAPTER 20

BY THE TIME the girls reached the woods behind the Dunmores' house, they were dirty and breathless. Rebecca's arms ached from holding the sleeping Kyle. They had run almost the whole way through the woods, stopping only to mark the way to the portal so they could find it again. Although they had still been able to follow the changeling's old trail with Tanya's black light, there was no sign of the creature anywhere. Rebecca was relieved; maybe it really had gotten away.

When they found Kawanna waiting for them

in the doorway, Clio checked her watch again. "Did they get back early?"

"Don't worry, Li'l Bit; you made it."

"We'd better get in there! We only have a few minutes to clean up before the Dunmores get back," Tanya said.

Kawanna patted her shoulder. "I told you girls not to worry. I took care of it. I figured it was the least I could do, since you were doing all the heavy lifting."

"Let's get Kyle changed and into bed," Rebecca said.

Maggie rushed ahead of them, and Rebecca heard her shout from the end of the hallway. "You guys! You won't believe it!"

When Rebecca arrived at the doorway, she was stunned to find that Kyle's room looked just the same as it always had, as though nothing had ever happened. "But . . . how?" she asked Kawanna.

"I don't know. Other than a knocked-over lamp, it looked like this when I got here."

"Maybe it's like that old theory of equilibrium," Tanya said. "The theory's been widely discredited, but maybe it makes sense in a supernatural context."

"In English, please?" Maggie said.

Tanya sighed. "Basically, nature likes balance. And the Night Queen disrupted nature. She had everything so out of whack that maybe when we defeated her, everything went back to how it was."

"Things will go back to normal for people, too, right?" Rebecca asked worriedly, looking down at Kyle. She placed him in his crib, and he reached for Bearbear, pressing his face into the soft, worn fur.

Just then, the girls heard the door open below. "We're home!" Mr. Dunmore called out.

"We're all upstairs!" Tanya answered. "Clio's aunt Kawanna got here a few minutes early. Kyle must have had a bad dream; he woke up not too long ago, so we're keeping him company."

Footsteps trooped up the stairs, and Mr. and Mrs. Dunmore appeared in the doorway. "Wow, all of you?" Mrs. Dunmore asked.

"I'm sorry; we just couldn't help it. He was just being so cute tonight!" Tanya said.

"Yeah, tonight's just one of those nights you don't want to let him out of your sight, you know?" Rebecca said.

The Dunmores bent over Kyle's crib, and Rebecca could feel their love for him like a physical presence in the room. "We know exactly what you mean," Mrs. Dunmore said.

Rebecca beamed. Kyle was home.

. . . . .

The next morning the friends sat in the costume shop sipping steaming cups of chamomile tea. Kawanna, dressed in a brilliant blue-and-vermillion silk robe, complete with fuzzy slippers shaped like monster feet, carried out a crystal cake stand loaded full of chocolate frosted cupcakes.

"Now we're talking," Maggie said, helping herself to the largest one. "Bring it on!"

"Are you sure, Mags? How do you know it won't turn into a big pile of worms?" Tanya teased.

"Don't remind me." Maggie took a huge bite

and pulled her head back in surprise as something long and wiggly dangled from her teeth. She screamed, spitting out the bite. The other girls pushed their cupcakes away in horror.

"Oops, I forgot to mention I put worms in these," Kawanna said. She reached into her pocket and flung a shower of colorful worms over the screaming girls. "Gummy worms!"

Clio scooped a handful of the candy from the floor and tossed it at her. "I swear, Auntie, one of these days!" She picked up her cupcake again. "There isn't anything else in here we should know about, is there?"

"That's it, Li'l Bit." Her eyes sparkled. "But you never know."

Rebecca took a cautious bite. "I think it's safe," she said. She sipped her tea. "You guys, what happened last night? I mean, I failed that last challenge. The Night Queen knew it, and I knew it. So why were we set free?"

Kawanna sat down next to the girls. "In books, *lusus naturae* are selfish creatures, capable of few emotions beyond amusement, greed, and cruelty.

They serve no one but themselves, and nothing gives them more pleasure than to twist the hearts of human beings. And I think that was the queen's plan for y'all. She hates to lose, so she wanted a way to win no matter what. If she could get you to harm the changeling, it would have put a cloud of darkness in your heart. Kyle may have been freed, but then you would have been hers. Maybe not right away, maybe not last night, but someday she would claim you for the Nightmare Realm. She was counting on it."

"Until Rebecca here decided to mess up her whole plan," Tanya said.

Maggie's mouth dropped open in indignation. "Wait a minute, you mean if we had played by the queen's rules, we would have lost no matter what?"

Kawanna nodded.

"Oh, man, I should have known," Maggie said, reaching for another cupcake. "Well, I definitely would have been toast. I was ready to put that little beast right out of its misery without a second thought."

"I don't know," Tanya said. "Do you think you

really would have been able to do it, if it came right down to it?"

"Luckily, we don't have to find out, because Rebecca wasn't having it," Clio said. "Apparently she's a heck of a lot more loving than the rest of us."

Kawanna poured more tea into her cup. "I don't know about all of that, but like my daddy used to say, 'If you don't like the rules, change the game.' Rebecca changed the game, and her compassion saved you. She was willing to risk sacrificing everything she loved the most, just for an unwanted changeling that had never shown her even a moment of love. That's pretty powerful." Rebecca felt her cheeks grow warm, and Kawanna smiled at her.

Clio stretched and stood up, picking up her plate. "Well, the important thing is we won. The Night Queen is stuck on her side of the portal for now, and once we find a way to seal it up for good, she won't be able to come back. She'll think twice before trying to mess with us again." She gathered up the other plates and carried them out of the room.

"I should get going," Rebecca said, rising to her feet. "I promised my parents I'd watch Isaac for a few hours while they go to the gym." She waved to the others and stepped through the shop's front entrance, the bell jingling brightly as the door swung open. There was something on the threshold. Rebecca bent down to pick it up. "Hey, Kawanna, there's something at the front door."

Kawanna walked over, and Rebecca handed her a scroll of paper tied with a scarlet silk ribbon. Kawanna untied the ribbon and slowly unrolled the scroll. There in immaculate calligraphy was one single word:

Remember.

Something fluttered to the ground at her feet.

It was the feather of a great horned owl.

Acknowledgments

Writing books is hard and scary, punctuated by crippling self-doubt, and there were so many wonderful humans (and dogs) that encouraged, inspired, critiqued, supported, and helped to make this book possible. First and foremost I would like to thank my magical unicorn of an agent, Erin Murphy, for knowing that I was a writer long before I knew it myself. Thank you one million times for believing in me. Huge and teary thanks to every member of the EMLA family for including me and welcoming me so warmly, even when I was just a lowly Plus One at my very first retreat. Being part of this community means so much to me, and I feel lucky to know every single one of you.

Heaps of thanks to my brilliant editor, Erin Stein, and the entire team at Imprint for bringing

Babysitting Nightmares into the world. Your insight, humor, and patience always remind me that this series has found the perfect home. To illustrator extraordinaire Rayanne Vieira, I am in awe of your artistic prowess and appreciative of your patience as you helped bring these girls out of my brain and onto the page.

Kirsten Cappy and Deb Shapiro, I thank you both for your insight, expertise, and joyful commitment to connecting books to readers. I'm fortunate to have you on my team. Deepest thanks to my two wise and thoughtful sensitivity readers; I am so grateful for your willingness to help me grow and improve. I loved the opportunity to learn from you, and I will keep striving to get it right. I am indebted to all of my early readers for their critiques: Sarah Azibo, Nicole Valentine, Lisa Robinson, Joyce Ray, Charlie Barshaw, and Martine Leavitt. Thank you for your time and kindness as we worked to make this book better.

Thanks also to the wonderful copy editors whose thorough precision saved my bacon on several occasions. Thanks also to Sarah Aronson for your support, guidance, and book bubbe goodness. Hugs and a huge high five for Claire Gunthert, my first kid beta reader, who gobbled this book up and wrote me my very first fan letter. Marvelous Claire, you are the reason writers write.

Thanks to all my friends and family, both on social media and IRL, who answered my questions, gave me encouragement, and shared their enthusiasm for my efforts. Extra-Special Thanks to Elly Swartz because I would never have finished this book without you. You are an incredible friend, and you cheered me on and helped me overcome every obstacle from Day One, even when I was working two jobs and had no time to write. For you my gratitude knows no bounds.

And finally, finally, FINALLY (which breaks our precedent because we always said you have to thank the spouse first!), I reserve my deepest and most bottomless thanks to my first, last, and best reader, my incredibly inspiring and supportive husband, Eddie Gamarra. You believed I could do it, so I did.

About the Author

KAT SHEPHERD is thrilled that her writing debut is a fast-paced story that is likely to engage reluctant readers, because as an educator, she believes that reading should be a joyful experience for every child.

She lives in Los Angeles with her husband, their two dogs, and a rotating series of foster dogs. Each year she and her husband travel to a different national park for their wedding anniversary, and they have been lucky enough to also visit places like South Africa, Paris, and the Galapagos Islands. Babysitting Nightmares is her first middle grade series.

katshepherd.com